LOVER'S KNOT

JENETTA JAMES

A Mysterious
Pride & Prejudice
Variation

Lover's Knot

ISBN-13: 978-1-5272-2078-2

Cover Image by CloudCat Design

❀ Created with Vellum

PRAISE FOR JENETTA JAMES

Suddenly Mrs. Darcy

"a touching, sometimes dark, often playfully sexy interpretation of what might have been" - Jane Austen's Regency World Magazine

"Jenetta James's writing made it incredibly easy for me to sink into Elizabeth's story and connect with her emotionally" - Austenprose

"Jenetta James is one of the most talented new JAFF writers of 2015. Emotionally charged, filled with a strong sense of voice and containing language that is both poetic in its delivery and precise in its meaning" - JustJane1813

"I enjoyed this story for its discerning premise, inventive intrigue, and beautifully developed romance! Ms. James is a skilled story-teller with a compelling voice and satisfying respect for Jane Austen's characters."- Austenesque Reviews

"...a fresh new story while recognizing and old favorite." - Delighted Reader Book Reviews

The Elizabeth Papers

"a novel that will appeal to fans of Jane Austen and romantic mysteries" - Publishers Weekly

"It will definitely be on my Best of 2016 list and is easily one of the best Pride and Prejudice inspired novels I have ever read." - Diary of an Eccentric

CONTENTS

PART I
THE DISCOVERY OF THE KNOT

CHAPTER 1

IN WHICH MISS ELIZABETH IS
SURPRISED AT DINNER AND MR. DARCY
TAKES CHARGE

The chill of the October air smacks my face and the beast thunders beneath me. His hooves throw clods of damp earth up and they whip through the air like so many stones. I let him have his head some time ago. My heart pounds, racing, and I am damp with hot sweat. Before me, at speed, the house emerges: red brick, pillar-fronted, and framed by field upon field of flat patchwork greens and browns. The harvest is long done, and the land lies fallow. I push myself harder, verging into pain. Suddenly, the animal lets out an unfamiliar sound by way of protest and I remember myself. My muscles tense and I pull the reins, losing speed, every moment. How can such energy, such fire, be gone so quickly?

Dusk is settling around me in its accustomed, creeping manner, falling like a veil before my eyes. Outside the house, a new carriage is stationed, a distracted coachman leaning against the door, eying his dusty boots. Another caller, no doubt. Another nondescript neighbour bearing greetings. Another anxious local mama in shameless pursuit of the Bingley fortune. A further unedifying spectacle among many. Not wishing to know any specifics of the scene, I make for the stables. The door to the kitchens is wide open, in spite of the weather. A pair of young maids are quietly bickering over a pail of water in the yard and a rotund man staggers into the property holding a dead pheasant aloft. The hollow crack of a shot sounds in the distance. Dismounting, I glance up at the rooms above. A figure moves away from a window so swiftly, I wonder whether it was ever there.

I have, not for the first time during my stay at Netherfield Park, the feeling of having just missed an event of some significance, of being on the edge of some hidden narrative, of being a spectator, who does not see. It is not a feeling that brings me comfort. A sudden longing for Pemberley, where every thing and every person is known, grips me. Bringing the reins to my right hand, without breaking step, I lead the horse along the gravel path. With my feet on the solid ground and my pace slow, I realise I am not fit to be seen. Mud splattered, sweat sodden, short of breath. The mounting dark shapes of my mind, of course, no man knows but me. Nevertheless, the avoidance of company and the privacy of my chamber are all I seek.

My rapid tread echoes round the hallway and I take the stairs two at a time. I have seen nothing of the ladies of the house or their guests. That is as I would have it. The very last thing I wish to behold is that wisp of patterned muslin on a young woman, moving quicker than she ought; a chestnut curl bouncing before me like a taunt. It is a relief to reach my chambers and find my valet, Stephenson, about some domestic task by the dimming light of the window. I nod to him in greeting as I enter and shed my coat like a used skin.

"Good ride, Mr. Darcy?"

There are men who would find him over-familiar, however, we have been together too long to object to the clandestine aspects of one another's characters. He is who he is, and so am I.

"Yes. Thank you, Stephenson. I went some distance beyond Meryton before turning back."

"You will have seen the country about then, sir? I reckon there is good fertile land here, albeit that the society may not be quite to your standards?"

His eyebrows rise. I refuse to be teased by my own valet.

"I am sure. I observed the militia moving in on my way out of the village." I paused. How many men had there been? I cannot say, but the memory of them surges through my mind. The roar of their march had sounded for miles, they appeared as a haze of slow moving red on the horizon as I galloped east. "Do you know anything of this?"

"They talk of little else below stairs, sir. There isn't a kitchen maid who is not agog with the notion of all the redcoats who shall be attending church on Sunday."

I could not but smile at this. Stephenson removes my boots with the practised proficiency I have come to expect from him. I disrobe and walk to my bath on the far side of the room, steaming, inviting. In the moment before I slice the water, I am ashamed to say, I think of her.

"Has anything been heard regarding either of the Misses Bennet?"

"I am given to understand that the elder Miss Bennet is still unwell, sir. She keeps to her bed, although Cook reports that she had some clear broth. As for Miss Elizabeth Bennet, I am told that she has passed most of the day attending to her sister but that she strolled in the gardens this afternoon where she was observed to stop for a time and read a book."

"Observed by whom?" I demand more rapidly than is wise. But I wish to know the answer. Are we dwelling in a house of spies? I do not care for the notion that she is being watched.

"Miss Bingley's maid told me, sir. She was doing some mending and saw it from the window. She just happened to mention it. It is fair to say that the girl is a regular gossip, sir. I do not believe her observation of the lady to be—deliberate." He did not look at me as he said this, which was for the best. At times, he is far more perceptive than he ought to be, but I acknowledge that trait has its uses.

"Thank you, Stephenson." He nods at this dismissal and departs, leaving me to myself.

Thereafter, I focus on my ablutions, in which the light and pleasing figure of Elizabeth Bennet plays no role.

My stay with Bingley and his family, which had ostensibly been arranged for his benefit rather than mine, has become increasingly burdensome. We had set out from our respective London homes only a se'nnight before, a cluster of carriages laden down with trunks, clattering north. My friend, who is an amiable and capable man, has long aspired to have a country estate to match his considerable wealth. To that end, he has leased this house and its lands. It has been my aim to assist him in establishing himself and arranging his affairs in the best possible manner. In consequence, I have applied myself most assiduously, and I hope, not in vain. The house is a fine prospect and the land about well husbanded and profitable. The village and the society, I cannot speak for. It has neither the familiarity of my native Derbyshire nor the sophistications of Town.

My confinement with Bingley's family has also been something of a trial. His two sisters, Mrs. Hurst and Miss Bingley, are my constant companions, tittering their assent to some opinion they assume me to have or disapproving of the local populace, loudly and at length. The attentions of Miss Bingley occasionally go further still. I should seek an ally in Bingley's brother-in-law, Hurst, were he ever away from his cups. I fear he is not. He is scarce about anything other than eating, drinking, shooting, or playing cards. He is given over, seemingly entirely, to the business of indulgence.

To this questionable ménage has been added the troubling attractions of the Bennet ladies. Miss Bennet and her sister Miss Elizabeth Bennet are the elder daughters of a local landowner. Their family appears to be one of the leading families of the area but that is to say little. All the evidence I have seen suggests to me that the life of the gentry hereabouts is confined and unvarying. In consequence, the Misses Bennet are considered the cream of the county. Not three miles from home, they are, nevertheless, currently residents at Netherfield on account of Miss Bennet having taken ill on a visit with Bingley's sisters and Miss Elizabeth Bennet walking hither to attend her. I do not pretend to comprehend a household whose young daughters roam the countryside alone and without protection, but there it is. The sight of Miss Elizabeth's skirts splattered with earth and her face flushed pink upon her arrival here enters my head, unbidden. I see her as she appeared that morning, in the drawing room, almond-shaped eyes smiling. Agitation begins to stir me, and the water feels warmer than before. Feeling foolish, I determine not to be so distracted and rise from my bath to dress.

~

Miss Elizabeth Bennet enters the saloon at Netherfield and smiles warmly, her eyes glittering. Hers is the sort of face that can reach into a man's mind and take up residence. The nature of her appearance goes quite beyond beauty, and she manages to shine with character. She wears a pale blue gown with a subtle pattern and her dark hair is arranged simply, I rather suspect by her own hand. Mrs. Hurst, who sits beside me on the chaise, clad from head to toe in silks and lace, takes out her eye-glass to observe the finer detail of the lady's appearance. For myself, I am quite content with the overall effect and turn away. My friend, and host, is more forthcoming.

"Miss Elizabeth, you look extremely well. May I enquire after the health of Miss Bennet?" Bingley stands and his head tilts. Worry is carved upon his face. He shows himself too freely and one day he shall rue it.

"Thank you, Mr. Bingley. She is rather poorly, but currently resting, so I am hopeful for the morrow. It is a great comfort to me that I am able to be with her, for which I thank you and Miss Bingley."

She nods towards her hostess who, at that moment gestures to a servant to offer Miss Elizabeth a glass of wine. Miss Bingley, sporting her third gown of the day, stands and takes the lady's arm as she speaks.

"You are most welcome, Miss Elizabeth. Please think nothing of it. What are neighbours for if not to proffer assistance in times of need? What manner of neighbour would I be if you were not to be made comfortable at your sister's bedside? It is such a shame that Miss Bennet chose to come on horseback. For, had she not been caught in the rain, she may not have fallen ill. Miss Bennet must consider herself a very accomplished rider to have declined the use of your father's carriage for the journey!"

She says nothing I do not think myself, but I smart at her speaking thus. I feel for Miss Elizabeth, although upon regarding her face, detect no symptoms of discomfort. Bingley, who sits beside Hurst, fidgets in his seat. If I know the man, he fears a scene but does not quite know how to prevent it. He has always struggled to contain his sisters. As it transpires, Miss Elizabeth is more than equal to the task of dealing with the matter herself.

"Well, it is but three miles, Miss Bingley. I do not consider it a *lengthy* journey on horseback or on foot. I cannot speak for my sister, but I like to feel the wind in my face and the movement of my person. There is enough sitting in this life, is there not?"

At that, Miss Bingley dropped her guest's arm and looks astounded. Maybe a little too astounded to be really convincing.

"How very bold of you, Miss Elizabeth! I cannot concur though. The open fields and the invigoration of the elements may be right for the gentlemen..."

With this she looks to me and I study my glass. I shall not be drawn into a discussion of manliness with Caroline Bingley. Seeming to realise that I will not reply, she laughs and continues. "But for a lady, the rewards of stillness and calm application cannot be over-valued. For is it not the tranquil arts in which a woman must excel if she is truly to be considered a lady?"

This barb only appears to produce a smile from its recipient.

"Miss Bingley, you have bested me. I fear I know not. Maybe I have not taken the trouble to examine how I may be truly considered a lady."

"Oh, Miss Bennet, I was not referring to you *expressly*. It was in general that I was speaking. Although, now that you mention it, no argument is ever compelling without an example. And the example who comes to my mind is our own Mr. Darcy's beloved sister."

"My sister?"

I bark the words and a knot of defensiveness forms within me. What does she know? How could she know? The knot tightens before I collect myself.

"Yes, dear Georgiana! For is she not the very definition of an accomplished lady? But her arts, Miss Bennet, are the mindful occupations of the interior life. She plays the pianoforte beautifully and studies languages and, no doubt, she sings. One day I should love to hear that."

With this wistful remark, her eyes fall upon me and she pauses. Her compliments to my sister are, for the most part, correct. But, as in all things, Caroline Bingley's knowledge is necessary but not sufficient for a proper understanding. She sees one edge of the picture but not the other, and thus makes a fundamental error.

"I thank you for that compliment to my sister, Miss Bingley, but I am afraid that I cannot quite accept it on her behalf. She is, as you say, an excellent pianist and will no doubt be a better one in time, with practise. She speaks French and Italian and reads quite widely for her age. These activities she pursues indoors as men and women alike generally do. Although, of course, there is nothing to stop any person reading out of doors in *clement* weather. Her singing is proficient rather than outstanding." I pause for a moment as the very act of speaking of my sister causes me to miss her. "Her horsemanship, however, is confident and elegant. It is the product of many hours of practice...*out* of the house."

I venture a glance to Miss Elizabeth and see her smile. No doubt she appreciates my support of her in this vulnerable moment. She is a young woman staying in the house of neighbours, far wealthier and better connected in society than she. It is quite unacceptable for Miss Bingley to suggest that she lacks femininity or accomplishment, and I shall not have it. The thought that I have assisted her, have eased her passage through the society of this evening, warms me.

Following a short interlude, in which the party briefly disperses, we assemble in the fine dining room and supper is served. I find myself beside Miss Elizabeth, keeping company with her subtle lavender scent. Her proximity is an unexpected occurrence. Quite against my better judgement, I find myself pondering her hands, the smooth skin of her arms, her unadorned neck, before stopping myself abruptly. I rake the recesses of my mind for some conversational gambit to end the silence, to avoid the unconscionable attractions of her bare skin beside me. I am about to ask about her reading when Mrs. Hurst enquires:

"Have your family always been settled in Meryton, Miss Elizabeth?"

"Yes." She looks up, beaming a smile of unaffected joy. "I was born at Longbourn, Mrs. Hurst, as were all my sisters. The estate has been in my father's family for many generations. And my mother is from a local family as well. Our uncle Philips is a solicitor in Meryton and his practice was my grandfather's before it was his. We are Hertfordshire natives and have many relatives here about."

Mrs. Hurst goes to speak further but her sister chimes in.

"I wonder that your family has not travelled further, Miss Elizabeth. After all, Hertfordshire is close to Town. Yet, Miss Bennet told us that your family rarely travels there except to visit your aunt and uncle in Cheapside. For myself, I could not be away from Town for so long, and it being an easy distance, intend to make the journey frequently."

"Well Miss Bingley, why should you not? If you have the resources and inclination and, as you say, the journey is not a great burden. I hope you will make all the journeys your heart desires, although I do not know how well your fondness for 'stillness' shall stand it."

It is not my practice to show amusement, except when among family and very close friends. But I must confess that the faintest laugh escapes my lips. Miss Bingley does not appear to notice and continues, unabashed.

"Possibly it is a difference in mentality between those who have grown up in the country and those who have been exposed to the sophistications of Town."

Fearful that she is about to make a positively offensive remark, I interject: "I doubt it, Miss Bingley. I grew up in the countryside but have not experienced an unwillingness to travel when the destination is worthy of it. What is more, I fear you overlook one aspect of great importance. That is, the benefits of long standing settlement in one place. My own family have lived in a settled location, away from Town, for many generations. That is to our advantage. I have the reassurance of knowing that I am acquainted with all around me. I know the circumstances of their fathers and grandfathers. I know where they live and where they came from. Their history, and mine, are things of record. In the throng of Town, no man can ever be sure of his neighbour."

It had occurred to me that Meryton, being close to Town and easily accessible on the road north, must be plagued with newcomers and travellers breaking their journeys. The market place, with its coaching inn and busy blacksmith, said as much. The town is a staging post on the way to and from London, a mark upon the road, attracting all manner of men, trouping through. Lambton does not suffer thus, which is as I would have it. As I sip my wine, Miss Elizabeth's voice springs up beside me.

"How very certain you are of your own particular knowledge, Mr. Darcy. But, is it not a false comfort? Is it not, at its heart, unrealistic? Many people find a move away from their place of birth unavoidable. There are the demands of family and enterprise. To say nothing of health and circumstance. Not all may be as fortunate as your family, or mine, and people must find their home where it presents itself. Sometimes, that place, may be a significant distance from where they started."

I tighten my grip upon my glass. My eyes find hers and, for one moment, I am drawn in utterly. She speaks, surely, of marriage. An arch look shoots towards me and her brow rises as she continues.

"It is quite impossible to ever have a full account of the people around us. There shall always be new arrivals, and they must always be welcome."

"Of course, and I would never fail to welcome newcomers to Pemberley. You misunderstand me, Miss Elizabeth. The reward of tradition and stability is knowledge. I know the society of my home. I am sure you know yours."

"Are you? How can you be certain? Does not every soul have its secrets?"

With that, I let the silence last too long and a blanket of discomfort steals around me. Her company holds me fast, like a pin on an entomologist's board. Suddenly aware that the table has fallen silent, and all eyes are fixed upon us, my mind races to find an answer. Even Hurst has paused his drinking. I reply as best I can: "I do not claim to know people's souls, Miss Elizabeth."

After a short interlude, the prattle of supper conversation and the click of cutlery on china re-commences. In this state, we continue until the meal is complete.

"Let us retire, ladies. The gentlemen must have their port and serious discussion." Miss Bingley does not look at her sister but squarely at Miss Elizabeth as she commands thus. She draws to her full, not inconsiderable height. Her fingers, like talons, she places on the edge of the table.

"No doubt they do, Miss Bingley. But, if I may be excused, I would check on my sister before joining you and Mrs. Hurst in the drawing room. I shall only be a moment." She looks questioningly but I wonder at her willingness to heed opposition. None comes, and Miss Elizabeth rises from the table, smiles sweeter than I believe she means, and departs the room in a sweep of her print gown. Her slim arms stretch out behind her as she moves into the darkened corridor.

Miss Bingley and Mrs. Hurst link eyes across the table and Miss Bingley exhales before turning to me.

"Well, really!"

With that, she begins to speak more discursively, and I must confess, I sip my wine and listen no longer. Bingley appears distracted and Hurst drains his glass before crashing it back down on the linen covered surface of the table. A servant moves to my left and begins removing plates. Footsteps sound from the passage beyond and a door in the middle-distance creaks.

Without warning, a scream breaks through the air like a splinter of glass. It smashes into the dining room without ceremony and eclipses all other sounds herein. It is the sort of sound to hit a man between the eyes and there is no time to react with noise of one's own. I know at once who it is and run from the table, Bingley behind me. Through the oak door, down the tiled corridor, closer, nearer to the ear splitting, bone shaking sound of her cry. The volume increases as I am close. In the foyer, I find nothing and turn down a small corridor which I believe leads to a narrow staircase up to Miss Bennet's chamber. It is a more direct route used by the maids. There is an equivalent one leading to the men's rooms, although I should never have taken it myself. My heart pounds in my chest as I round the corner and race along the echoing passage, seeing her immediately.

Miss Elizabeth. Hunching over the crumpled form of a man. Plainly dead.

"Miss Elizabeth! Please, step back."

I rush up behind her, reaching for her creamy shoulders on instinct. Her face, as it turns to me, is colourless, stunned. Her eyes blink and her lips quiver almost imperceptibly. Upon the uneven floor is the figure of a man, a servant, with a blade through his chest and a lake of blood around his person. It kisses the edge of Miss Elizabeth's slippers, pale blue no longer. Without thinking, I clasp her upper arms and she protests not as I move her away. Her bearing, silent, rather wooden, stirs me to hold her, but I cannot.

Bingley begins issuing orders, calling out for servants. His bellows of "lock the doors" and "secure the house" boom out, a voice unlike his own. His arms jerk around and before long people appear—the butler, footmen, young maids—quickly shooed away. My eyes search for Stephenson until he appears at the top of the stairs and he descends towards the multitude. As the portly figure of Hurst bounds towards us, his wife and Miss Bingley close behind, shrieking enquiries, the man of the house begs the ladies away from the scene. He is, sadly, not swift enough. Miss Bingley and her sister burst into the passage and together, observing the horror, begin to wail. Bingley attempts to restore calm.

"Caroline, please escort Miss Elizabeth back to the drawing room. I shall have servants attend you. You will remain there. Do not depart the room."

A look of horror chases across Miss Elizabeth's face. Her mouth opens but no words come out. I speak quiet, direct to Bingley.

"I suspect Miss Elizabeth would like to see her sister. She also requires a change of shoes."

She throws me a look, not wholly cold, and something inside me clenches. Mrs. Hurst runs from the room, silks trailing, sobbing loudly. Her husband follows and Miss Bingley looks to her brother, her hands shaking. I note that she has not dissolved entirely and determine to use that to the benefit of others.

"Miss Bingley, might I suggest that you accompany Miss Elizabeth to Miss Bennet's chamber? My valet Stephenson"—I nod to him and he moves closer, watchful, single-minded—"shall remain without. I recommend you lock the door."

Her eyes follow mine to Stephenson standing a few steps above us. Wordlessly, she complies. Miss Bingley steps forward, offering Miss Elizabeth her arm and ascends the stairs with Stephenson following close behind.

When I turn to Bingley, panic is rising in him like steam from a pot. It occurs to me that we have trouble enough without the gentleman of the house losing his head.

"Bingley, I suggest we summon the magistrate." My friend stares at the sight before him and gulps. "He visited you this week, a Mr. Allwood. His estate is north, on the road to Hitchen. Somebody should ride out there without delay. I would offer to go myself, but I rather think it our responsibility to stay here to secure the safety of the ladies…"

I look to his face for a response. It is not in my nature to wait for others, so I continue to deal with matters as I see them.

"Perhaps that young man in the stables, Jonny? He is a good rider and appears trustworthy. He is local. He'll know where he is going in the dark. Send him with a letter. The weather is still poor but that cannot be helped. We could send to Meryton for the constable, but I question the value of that. You have had all of the doors locked. That is good. I propose that you and I go round the house and personally check that the thing is done and a male member of your service be appointed to sit by each door on the inside until the arrival of Mr. Allwood."

The butler, Wilkins, vigorously nods as does another beside him, whom I take to be a senior footman. It occurs to me that we ought to be able to count upon Hurst in this matter. He is a gentleman and a member of the family—dash it—but, where is he? Filling his goblet, no doubt.

"Now, who is this poor unfortunate soul?"

For the first time, I study the creased face upon the floor and an ache inside me hardens. He wears the uniform of the household and his fists are clenched. He appears, even in the gruesome and chaotic manner of this discovery, to be tall and fairly slim. His face is young, and he has a broad forehead, framed by ash blond hair. The sight of that face, inert and upon the floor, fetches a half-remembered image to my mind, but I cannot place it. I have no doubt noticed him at some unremarkable moment of his life, during the weeks I have been at Netherfield.

The dependable Wilkins steps forward, and, although it is not his usual habit, speaks with a stutter: "His n—name is—was Partridge, sir. Tom P—partridge. He was an under footman. T—taken on, only this week from the village."

"A footman you say? But he was not, unless I am mistaken, serving at dinner?"

"No, sir. He was down to cover dinner tomorrow. I had tasked him with checking Mr. Bingley's breakfast service and setting the break-fast table."

The small dining room, in which all of the household, save Mrs. Hurst, broke their fast is on the other side of the house and I know for fact that the passageway in which we are assembled, is not a route to the kitchens. Inwardly, I query how the chap had come to be in this particular place, a small corridor with a side staircase close to the main hall, leading to the ladies' chambers above.

"I see. Do you know, Wilkins, what may have brought him to this particular spot?"

"I have n—no idea, Mr. Darcy."

Bingley, who has been staring at the deceased man for some time, straightens and appears to come to.

"Darcy, whatever are we to do with him? We cannot leave the fellow here!"

"I quite agree. But I do not think Mr. Allwood would thank us for moving the victim before his arrival. I suspect he shall wish to see him *in situ*. However, that being done, he must indeed be moved elsewhere."

"Yes, of course, of course," mutters Bingley. "I shall write a note to this Allwood immediately—I shall do it now and return directly."

With this pronouncement, he darts off in the direction of the drawing room and I turn to Wilkins, whom I have always considered a sensible man.

"This is a shocking business, Wilkins, and I fear that we may do little until Mr. Allwood arrives. Let us concentrate on securing the house and its inhabitants." I pause and think of the party upstairs. "Wilkins, it occurs to me that special efforts ought to be taken to protect the ladies. What are the ways of reaching the corridor of their chambers?"

"Only three, Mr. Darcy, sir. Up this staircase, up the main staircase, and by way of the servants' quarters. There is a door from the back staircase that comes out opposite Miss Elizabeth Bennet's chamber. That is where the maids come up in the mornings."

"Right. Thank you, Wilkins. I feel that if Mr. Bingley were here he would say this himself, but I rather think that the bottom of each of those staircases should be guarded by a member of the staff. No doubt there will be panic in the servants' quarters before long, but I am quite sure that you shall be able to quell that. The female servants must feel safe in their beds. For the men of the house, I suspect that it shall be a long night."

"Quite so, Mr. Darcy, quite so."

At this moment, Bingley returns, and his letter is dispatched with the surly-faced Jonny into the dark, rain-sodden night. I inform my friend of the discussions that have taken place in his absence and he concurs with my suggestions.

"Very good, Darcy, absolutely. But, well, there is one thing, and—well…the fact is that we have no idea who has done this appalling thing, or why, or…where that person may be now. If he is now beyond the house, then all well and good. Or rather, not all well and good but as well as can be expected and obviously, locking the place up and guarding it will keep the villain at bay. Problem is, Darcy, what if he is still here?"

He looks around him. The light of the candles is dying down around us, the remaining servants are respectfully covering the late Tom Partridge with a great sheet of linen fetched a moment before by a sobbing girl.

"What if he is…good god…on the inside? What if by pulling up the drawbridge, we are locking the fellow in?"

I had underestimated Bingley and resolve not to do so again. It is, of course, a risk, but I can see no alternative.

"You may be right, but what else can be done, Bingley? We have to assume that he is not still in the house and act accordingly. In the unlucky event that he is still in here, well he would be most unwise to do anything."

"But he may be a madman, Darcy!"

"He surely *must* be a madman, but if he is still in the house then let us pray he is a madman who does not wish to be apprehended. We must hold the fort until the arrival of the magistrate, guard your sisters and guests, and maintain the safety of the household."

He agrees, and we act accordingly. We inform the ladies, who are now subdued, of this plan and they assent. I see at once that Miss Elizabeth has changed her gown and slippers and is wearing a shawl I believe to be Miss Bingley's. My heart is grateful for this small token of kindness, for the night is already an unhappy one. If I could thank Miss Bingley for this act of charity, without appearing to show an excess of interest in the second Miss Bennet, then I would do so. Instead, I remain silent.

The hours of the night slouch past us like old dogs. Bingley and I sit on incidental chairs, placed in the carpeted hallway and perfectly spaced between the doors to the chambers of Miss Bingley and the two Miss Bennets. Hurst, who appears sometime after Bingley's note was dispatched to the magistrate, reports that his wife is suffering an attack of nerves on account of events and it is agreed that he would do better to stay with her. I cannot consider this a loss. Hurst cannot reliably remain awake during the day, so he can be of little help to us on our long night watch. I sit in silence, watching the shadows falling in the hall, listening for any creak, any whisper in the emptiness. Bingley and I have agreed not to speak, lest we wake the ladies, but we exchange the odd hushed greeting in the slow hours of our duty. I will not allow myself to fall into slumber although every part of my body cries out for rest. Periodically, Stephenson, who is patrolling the house, fetches me a cup of water or a hot coffee. We, none of us, know how long it will take Jonny in the lashing rain and howling winds to get to Mr. Allwood nor how long it will take them both to make the return journey.

The clock in the hall chimes out the hours. The darkness of the night sits weighty on our shoulders and my mind meanders to places it should eschew. The wonders of that chamber at my back, *her* chamber, I imagine in the many idle moments of my watch. The nearness of her person behind the solid door, the room within, cocooning her. Shuttered into darkness, the vast bed, laid heavy with blanket and counterpane and the curly, chestnut head deep in slumber against the deep down of the pillow. These thoughts, I taste, savour, and then sweep away. Some of them are not entirely worthy of me. I remind myself that Miss Elizabeth Bennet is a maiden and a gentleman's daughter, and my task at this moment is to protect her as I would my own sister. In the silence, I smile remembering her remarks earlier in the evening, at the ease and fluency of her responses, at her self-assured profile listening, unconvinced, to others. Despite the hour and my lack of rest, I am anxious to return to that exchange, even the challenges. How odd that I should think of the pleasures of conversation with a girl of no consequence rather than the matter at hand.

CHAPTER 2

IN WHICH MR. ALLWOOD ARRIVES AT NETHERFIELD AND MISS ELIZABETH MISUNDERSTANDS MR. DARCY

The hour is close to six, and dawn is near when Jonny reappears with Mr. Allwood. The clunk and shift of maids arriving with mops and fire materials has been underway for some time. Sleepless and bone-weary, I stand at the sound of the great door opening and the tread of new feet upon the stone floor. Anxious that the ladies should not rouse earlier than necessary, I whisper to my friend, "Bingley? I believe Mr. Allwood is here."

He straightens with a jolt, snorts somewhat, and, no doubt forgetful of our vow of quietness pronounces loudly, "Bloody good thing too!"

An hour or so later, the gentlemen and Wilkins gather in Bingley's study to examine matters. Mr. Allwood has made an inspection of the dead man and suggests immediately that his body be moved to the game larder. The thing is done, and the two young women charged with cleaning up the scene of his demise clank into the hall with buckets full of water and cloth hung over their shoulders. They appear to me to be excessively young girls to have been given such a grisly task, but so it is. I am not without sympathy for them and make a study of their faces as they begin their work. What do I see? Horror, certainly, and quite possibly disgust. Apart from this, I observe no real emotion and wonder why. For is it not the case that although every person present is shocked to their core, not one has come forward as this man's friend? Who was Tom Partridge and who were his intimates?

"Mr. Bingley, I can only commend your handling of the events of last evening. I could hardly have done better had I been here myself."

Mr. Reginald Allwood, gentleman and magistrate, is a spindly vision, his bones seeming to jut from his respectable frock coat, his greying fair hair sitting on his head like a thatch on a stick. His eyes, one can hardly forget. They are green and ever on the move. As to dress and the particular aspects of his deportment, he is not so far distant from his Hertfordshire brethren. He appears to lack that polish which is the product of passing time with the highest in society. Frankly, I remain to be convinced of his abilities. And yet, there is nothing for it but to trust the man and obey the law.

"As you have no doubt deduced, and as you no doubt would wish, the murderer may be far from here by now. If that is the case, then it is my duty to gather what information I can and pass it to neighbouring magistrates. We are sufficiently close to Town that I shall also send information to Bow Street, although I would rather not be reliant on their offices. They have their uses, mercenary adventurers that they are, and the crime is so serious that I fear we must do all within our powers."

He sips from the coffee he has been given and glances around the room, peering at each of us in turn as a cat may regard a mouse. To be a guest in another man's home is trial enough but to be a guest in another man's home and be examined critically by the local magistrate is quite another. My mind leaps to Pemberley. To the comforts of my own chamber, to the familiar smell of my own library, lit by its great fire, to the sunlit, mist coated undulations of the estate folding out as far as the eye can see. Unaware of my reverie, Mr. Allwood continues with every appearance of confidence.

"Mr. Bingley, I note that you are a newcomer to this part of the world. Do you have any knowledge of the dead man?"

"I regret almost none, sir, save his name and position. I believe that Mr. Wilkins, our butler here at Netherfield, may be better placed to provide further information." Bingley looks to Wilkins who takes a deep breath and speaks in a manner, I must say, rather rehearsed.

"Mr. Allwood, sir, Tom Partridge was taken on here as an under footman one week ago. He did not travel with the Bingley household from Scarborough, whence Mr. Bingley is come, but was hired locally. We have taken on a number of local people since the household was established, from outlying villages. He was one such. He came to the door to apply for a position, was interviewed, appeared satisfactory, and was taken on."

"Where was he from?"

"His parents are tenant farmers out Gosmore way, sir. He is a younger son in a family of five and had worked as a boot boy and an under footman at an estate some distance from here. Wishing to better himself, he came to Netherfield."

"Has a message been sent to his family?"

Bingley, who had previously appeared redundant, came forth with a reply: "It was dispatched this morning, sir, with the dawn."

"I see. And can you tell me how he performed his duties?"

"Perfectly well, sir. I saw nothing amiss and nothing was reported to me."

"And what was he like, Mr. Wilkins? How did he appear to others?"

"I am not sure as I can say, sir. Seemed a perfectly ordinary sort of man. He went about his duties, he conversed with his fellow servants in spare moments. I believe he walked into the village on his evening off. He appeared a regular sort of cove, if you know what I mean, sir?"

Allwood looks blank and replies quietly. "I know nothing that you gentlemen have not told me. Is there anything else about this man that any person present can recall about his manner or activities whilst alive?"

Hurst, Bingley, and I all reply in the negative. Even as I speak, the nagging finger of regret pulls on my arm. For had I not, as I beheld the man's countenance, thought I recalled something? I rack my memory for the root of it but find nothing and "nothing" is not the answer the magistrate seeks. Wilkins begins to shuffle his feet upon the carpeted floor.

"Is there something further, Wilkins?" Bingley asks in a gentle tone.

"Well, it is probably of no import, sir... It is only—that one of the kitchen maids mentioned to the cook that she found his accent ... peculiar."

"Peculiar?"

"Could not place it, sir. I remembered because the girl in question is a local hire. She is from Meryton, so I thought it odd that she did not know his accent, which I took to be a local one."

Could such a piece of kitchen prattle be important? What one young woman below stairs thinks of a man's way of speaking, could that enable others to understand his death? I lean back in my chair, considering the whole approach of Mr. Allwood to be rather fanciful. For his part, the magistrate falls silent for a moment and runs his finger over his chin as though he is expecting to find more there.

"I see. Quite interesting. Thank you, Mr. Wilkins. Do you recall the name of the girl?"

"Mildred, sir. I shall ask the housekeeper to provide her family name."

"I am grateful. I shall set up in here if that is acceptable to you, Mr. Bingley?" He looks to my friend, who, for a moment looks about, as if there is another Bingley present in the room. "I shall start by interviewing the family and then move onto the servants—"

Horrified, I interject. "Mr. Allwood, I am afraid there is a problem. Firstly, two of the family are ladies, already distressed and with no information that could possibly be useful. Secondly, and more pressingly, there are two female guests in the house. Miss Bennet is the daughter of a neighbouring gentleman. She has been unwell and kept to her bed for the past day and certainly during the dreadful events of last night. She is surely too unwell to be questioned in any event. Her sister, Miss Elizabeth Bennet, is also a guest here and was the unfortunate lady who discovered the crime. We could not allow you to interview her without her father present—"

"Well, send for him then."

Beside me, Hurst emits an indeterminate, gruff noise. "His first daughter arrived on horseback, wet through, and his second came forth, up to her knees in mud having walked, so god knows how we are to expect the father!"

My throat tightens. It is not for Hurst to refer to Miss Elizabeth's knees.

"He has a carriage, Hurst. I observed it at the assembly. I know not why it did not convey either of his daughters, but it exists."

"In any event, I shall take mine to Longbourn personally and escort Mr. Bennet to Netherfield," interjects Bingley. "This dreadful event has taken place while his daughters were under my roof, and I should be the one to inform him."

My friend having departed, I make for his library. Opening the great oak door onto the leather-lined, flame-flickered space within, I am astonished to see Miss Elizabeth look up from a seat by the fire. The orange light dances on her face and falls softly on the fabric of her gown. She holds in her small hands a book, half read. The white flesh of her left foot, glows before me. I recall the feeling of her arm beneath my hand only the previous evening and feel myself pinned to the door. I have, in my life, seen more than the bare flesh of a woman's foot. And yet this sight suspends me. After a moment of seeming hesitation, she shifts the fabric of her gown to conceal the wink of flesh, smiles slightly and bids me good morning. The ordinary formality of her manner, brings me back to myself.

"Good morning, Miss Elizabeth. May I?"

I take up a book, discovered the previous day, and as she nods, sit on the chaise neighbouring her chair. Here we remain, in silence, for some time. Her proximity reminds me of the long night just passed in reveries of her. I begin to feel rather hot. This cannot continue.

"Miss Elizabeth, may I enquire what you are reading?"

"Certainly, Mr. Darcy. I am enjoying 'Evelina' by Frances Burney. Have you read it?"

"I have. It is a classic, as is 'Cecelia'. Do you read novels generally?"

"I suppose I do, although not exclusively. I also read histories. I have even been known to experiment with philosophies. I try to read as widely as I am able, Mr. Darcy."

"Inside and out?"

She looks up and her eyes spark like matches. "Yes." She laughs, and I feel suddenly lighter having drawn that response from her. "But not today." She inclines her head towards the window, currently lashed by the rain. The water forms a hazy impenetrable skin on the glass. "My sister sleeps and for some relief, I read here rather than in her chamber. I hope that I have not invaded your own sanctuary?"

"Certainly not, Miss Elizabeth." I wish to say more, but words desert me. Her shiny curls turn back to the page and the moment is lost. I stare, unseeing, at my own page and grow impatient for progress.

"Miss Elizabeth, I hope that you are not too distressed by the events of last evening? You are quite safe now. The house is very well guarded, and Mr. Bingley is for Longbourn to your father."

"Thank you, Mr. Darcy. I am quite well." She looks solemn. "I observed Mr. Bingley's carriage departing from Jane's window. But I did not know his destination. I am worried, sir, that my sister is not yet well enough to return home."

"I do not believe that is the purpose of his visit. The magistrate, Mr. Allwood, arrived this morning, Miss Elizabeth. And he...well, he is likely to wish to speak with you."

"I see. Of course." With this, she stares into the burning glow of the fire. "Mr. Allwood is known as a formidable man in this part of the country, Mr. Darcy. And somewhat of an enigma. Should I quake at my questioning, do you think?"

"I hope not. Do you quake at anything?"

"I assure you, I do. I quake at events such as that last evening."

"Of course. I did not mean to be flippant. As to Mr. Allwood, I imagine your interview with him shall be of short duration, as of course, it should be."

"Should it?"

"Of course."

"Why?"

"Why?" At this question, I am incredulous. "Because you are a gentleman's daughter and you have had horror enough. You were in an unfortunate place at an unfortunate time and are an innocent who can have no information apart from that already known. I accept that he must speak to you. But he ought to be circumspect about what he may learn. And frankly, my view is that he should leave you and Miss Bennet and the ladies of the house in peace."

"Do you think that the ladies should be excused from truth telling then, Mr. Darcy?"

"I did not say that."

"You suggested it though. I cannot agree, I am afraid. My own analysis is that a terrible crime has been committed, and we must all assist. I cannot say that I should be questioned less critically or less thoroughly because I am a gentleman's daughter."

The lightness that had warmed me before is gone from her face. My mind races to keep up with her changing attitude.

"It is not about the obligation to tell the truth, Miss Elizabeth. That rests on you as it rests on us all. And you shall no doubt dispatch it fully, as shall I. It is not that. It is about you and Miss Bennet, as innocent bystanders with very little information, being treated as respectfully as possible."

"I thank you for your solicitousness, Mr. Darcy, and for the steps that you and Mr. Bingley have taken to ensure the safety of the house. But I ought also to be clear with you. I am not the sort of young lady who requires to be sheltered like a rare orchid in a sharp breeze. I have no pretensions to the sort of femininity that consists in closing my eyes to the truth or to the moral compass that compels us all."

Her eyes glow fiercely, drawing me closer. Without knowing it, I have moved and find myself on the edge of the chaise, leaning towards her, searching for words. At that moment, the door opens, and a maid bobs a curtsy.

"Miss Elizabeth, Mr. Bennet has arrived. He is waiting for you in the drawing room."

A smile breaks across her face and she stands. As she leaves the room in the maid's wake, she says, "Goodbye, Mr. Darcy," without even looking back.

In her absence, I cannot simply sit. On my feet, I pace the room for some time, considering the rain-drenched carriage outside the window and recall the lightness of her figure as she had departed. I can make no sense of my time with her. She has a way of assuming opinions I do not possess, of catching my words erroneously. At the same time, we have been alone in this room, by the fire, among the pages. And she has looked me squarely in the face, as a person who may have known me all my life might. She does not demure from challenge as some ladies would. She smiles and even laughs. I cling to the memory of that laugh and the knowledge that I alone elicited it.

My own interview with Mr. Allwood was somewhat unsatisfactory and I have since examined and re-examined it a number of times. I was taken aback by his beginning. Rather than asking for my reflections on the previous evening, he commenced by asking me about myself. Unaccustomed as I am to being interrogated, but aware that a grave crime had taken place, I endeavoured to assist. In short order, I related a basic account of myself including my parents being late of the world, my guardianship of my beloved sister, and my ownership of Pemberley.

"You are a man of means, Mr. Darcy, am I correct?"

"You are."

"I am obliged to you for your lack of prevarication."

I nodded in response and then gave an account of various matters. When Mr. Allwood asked me how I had travelled to Netherfield, I answered that I had my own carriage but that I had departed London simultaneously with the Bingley party, including Mr. and Mrs. Hurst. It felt like yesterday, but how the time between then and now has concertina'd and raced past us. The magistrate settled his green-eyed stare straight at me and absently stroked the arm of his chair as I spoke. Thereafter, I gave as detailed a chronicle of the previous day as possible, including my ride, the household assembling in the saloon, and the dinner itself.

"You said, Mr. Darcy, that between assembling for drinks in the saloon and sitting down to supper, the party briefly dispersed. Where did you go?"

"I remained in the saloon."

"Alone?"

"Yes."

"Where did the others go?"

"I believe that the ladies retired to their respective chambers. Miss Elizabeth Bennet may have visited her sister, but I am speculating. Bingley wished to speak to Wilkins about a staff matter and took Hurst with him."

"And you did not think to take yourself off somewhere, Mr. Darcy."

"No. I am not disposed to be uncomfortable in my own company. I did not anticipate the party being absent for long, and I was right. I would say that within fifteen minutes, the ladies returned, and thereafter, the gentlemen."

"I see. Did anyone else come into the room while the others were gone?"

"No."

Mr. Allwood asked more questions, I answered him, and he thanked me. Realising that I was dismissed, I sought to leave the room without display of my feelings. Where was Miss Elizabeth? Was she to be probed as I had been, and *doubted,* too? It was my strongest inclination to sit beside her while she answered the magistrate's questions, but that, I acknowledged, was the role of a father or a husband. I stormed out of the house to the stables, heedless of the driving, icy rain and howling winds, seeking relief from my own mind.

~

Although he is invited to remain for supper, Mr. Allwood declines, in favour of a cold, wet ride back to his own estate. It is agreed that he would return the next morning and continue his discussions with the servants, which he has not completed. To my knowledge, the magistrate has met with all of the family: Mrs. Hurst and her husband being interviewed together, and Bingley sitting with Miss Bingley during the ordeal. Miss Elizabeth Bennet was accompanied by her father and the elder Miss Bennet was, quite properly, spared. I understand from Miss Bingley that Miss Bennet is still unwell and her sister has not informed her of the terrible events for fear of upsetting her health. Mr. Allwood has worked with remarkable speed to speak with not only those named but also the main body of the household's servants. I watched them go in and I watched them go out. He spent considerable time with Wilkins, the housekeeper, Mrs. Potter, and Molly, one of the maids.

Prior to his departure, he gathers Bingley, Hurst, and me together by way of drawing the day to a close. To my knowledge, the man has not eaten, having declined nuncheon, and has been served only coffee. He appears no different than he had that morning, and I begin to wonder at his constitution.

"Gentlemen, I shall return in the morning. I have had a good many useful discussions. Upon the morrow, I shall complete my interviewing of the servants. This"—he held out a sheet of paper before returning it to his person—"is a list of people I believe to have visited here yesterday. It includes a number of tradesmen, a Mr. and Mrs. Long, who called upon Mr. Bingley and his sister, and a Mr. Philips, a local solicitor who met with Mr. Bingley's agent to discuss a right of way across the land. All of those named, I have requested attend here tomorrow."

Bingley responded, a certain matter clearly praying on his mind: "I am glad to hear it, Mr. Allwood. May I ask... What am I to do with the dead man's body, sir? I am conscious of the need to bury him, but of course, there shall be an inquest. As you know, his family has been

28

notified and I have also sent a message to the rector of the church in Meryton. However, I—"

"Yes, yes. I understand you. Have I finished examining the body? Yes. The physician has seen him. There is nothing to learn there except to say that he was stabbed once—with some precision. Whether that was luck or judgement, we cannot presently know. I believe he died very quickly and that he was murdered in exactly the place he fell. In my estimation, he died between one and two hours before he was found; hence, there is Mr. Bingley, no call to maintain his body in the larder. It may be appropriately dealt with at the inquest, and then…" His voice dies, and he moves his hands by way of expression. He need not say more. I know perfectly well that bodies are usually displayed at the inquest prior to being buried.

"However, that brings me to another matter. A matter most material which has just come to light. The messenger, who was sent to convey news of this affair to the dead man's parents, returned without having found them and so, I sent a runner of my own. That man has now reported back to me, and I am afraid to say that there are no Partridges at Gosmore. There is a Wood Box Farm at Ickleford, but the tenants there are a young couple and they have never heard of our man or any other person answering to his description."

Mr. Allwood, having delivered this news, looks up at each of us. My friend Bingley is, I sense, worrying about what this means for the disposal of the dead man's remains after the inquest has been completed. Hurst, who has been growing impatient, no doubt for his evening repast, begins to grumble that it does not matter a fig. I consider whether he may be right. After all, should the magistrate not be looking for the murderer rather than concerning himself to such a degree with the victim? On the other hand, if we cannot even identify the victim, however shall we find his killer? The sight of the dead man's face returns to me. The oddness of this affair pricks my skin like a needle. *Stand back and think, man!* A servant, whom it appears now was an imposter, has been brutally murdered in the home of a gentleman in the middle of dinner. The assailant commits the crime in a place where it would be quickly discovered and then vanishes. In the chaos and confusion, I have underestimated the sheer strangeness that surrounds me. For the moment, I am content to give Mr. Allwood the benefit of the doubt. The man himself, continues.

"And so, gentlemen, having started the day with one mystery, we now have two. Firstly, who was the man calling himself Tom Partridge? Allied to that, why did he inveigle himself into Mr. Bingley's household on the basis of a false identity? Secondly, who killed him, why, and where is that person now?" He raises his eyebrows in the closest approximation to a smile that has graced his face since his arrival. "I shall see you gentlemen in the morning."

He makes for the door and I think of Miss Elizabeth sitting with her sister.

"I assume that you have completed your discussions with all parties, save those named on your list, sir?"

"Never assume anything, Mr. Darcy," Allwood says over his shoulder as he departs the room.

CHAPTER 3

IN WHICH AN INQUEST TAKES PLACE

*M*r. Allwood's visits to Netherfield continue for a further two days and proceed much the same as before. I am surprised to learn that the Mr. Philips whom he has summoned is the attorney uncle of the Misses Bennet. That gentleman shuffles into Bingley's study like a top-hatted sloth and is there for some time. On his way in, he introduces himself to me in a rather forward manner, offers his limp hand, and inclines his head. He enquires as to whether I intend to return to Derbyshire in the near future, which I consider to be odd as well as rude. Of course, I did not answer. Then he seeks my opinion on the Americas and I begin to think there are no limits to eccentricity in this corner of the world. Frankly, so many things are not as they usually are that I do not dwell on his conduct for long. It does not escape me that Miss Elizabeth does not seek out her uncle whilst he is at Netherfield. Despite having been told by a maid that Mr. Phillips was in the drawing room, Miss Elizabeth keeps to her sister's chamber and is not seen to venture out. Is she so embarrassed by her family that she maintains a distance from them even in such circumstances as these? In any event, if Allwood learns anything of value from this oddity, he does not impart it to Bingley or me.

The dead man is handed over to the authorities, the house is restored to some semblance of order, and the whole business diminishes in a haze of frustration and ignorance. The routines each evening for securing the house are made stricter; it has emerged that prior to the murder, they were alarmingly negligent. Allwood claimed that there is a total of four doors to the house which, prior to the murder, had been routinely left unlocked at night. He did not add, because it was not necessary, that any person in the county could have gained access to the house on the night in question. Bingley and Wilkins work assiduously to reassure the household, above and below stairs.

Unquestionably, the atmosphere has changed. The ways of thinking and doing that pervaded the household have shifted. Upon returning from my ride one morning, I observe a maid of all work drop an empty pail upon the hard floor of the back corridor. The other servants present shriek, fairly jumping out of their wits in alarm. I fancy that they represent the tattered nerves of the house in general.

I attempt in a private moment with Mr. Allwood to understand what he has gleaned; however, I find him as guarded as ever and learn nothing. As he departs the house, he touches his hat and says he is to dine with the colonel of the regiment. That most singular man, atop his horse, was halfway down Bingley's drive before I recall the presence of the militia so near. What a fool I have been, not to think of this as significant.

My hessians click on the tiled floor of the hall at Netherfield when I come in from a cold ride. I move swiftly, as I always have done. My mind smiles to recall my sister skipping after me. "Slow down, Fitzwilliam! I cannot keep up." The truth is, I have no place for slowness, at home or abroad. That click of my boot, like an affirmative action, a confirmation that I know where I am going. My body is taut, and my senses heightened. In the middle distance, I hear one hand of a sonata on the pianoforte and a woman's voice. Servants undertaking daily tasks and wearing harried expressions appear in corners. Bingley laughs uproariously in another room. A fire in the grate crackles as a girl throws another log on it. Still I move forward, past oil paintings and great tapestries in one hundred colours, swirling in the corners of my vision. I have the idea that if I can move quicker still, I may understand matters better. The Bingleys and the Hursts are here in the house, but I do not think of them. The dark panels of the library door appear before me, and I slow before opening it in one swift movement.

Within resembles another world, a warmer world. The fire blazes, throwing orange light around the book-lined room. Shadows dance on the walls like spirits and my mind feels oddly light. The place is perfectly ordered, save for one aspect. In the centre of the room, atop a silken chaise, lies Miss Elizabeth Bennet. A calm hangs about her form and a stillness, her beauty resting. Her skin glows luminous in the fire light and her soft, full breasts rise and fall in the deep breathing of her sleep. My eyes linger there, for I hardly believe that I am allowed this moment in her presence. Her left foot is not quite on the floor, its flesh peeping out from the muslin of her gown. A book, half-read, is held loosely in her right hand. I imagine her eyes gently shutting in slumber, forgetful of the pages.

My heart pounds in my chest and having been first pinned to the door, I am released and move forward. I have been brought up to expect a particular manner of life, for those around me to behave in a particular way. But nothing is as it seems at Netherfield. It is as though the ordinary world has stopped like a clock and nothing is beyond imagining.

I move closer to her and whisper her name. She speaks not, but I can smell her sweet, lavender scent. Somewhere behind me, deep in the house, the dinner bell rings and a door opens. My chest tightens as I regard her sleeping form. "Elizabeth?" Still, she answers not. I kneel beside her and the heat from the fire sears my side. What could be more intimate than to watch a woman sleep, dark lashes laid heavy against creamy skin? I edge closer still and everything, save for her, recedes. Boldness streaks though me, and with it, a determination to obtain the happiness I seek. She does not wake at my speaking her name, so I lean in and kiss her lips.

An icy hand grips my heart as it thuds harder. Those lips, which were berry red, are pale and cold beneath my own. The lavender scent is still there but faint. I feel her slipping away from me like a memory from long ago, but I cannot allow it to continue. "Elizabeth? Elizabeth?" Louder and louder and more frantic comes my voice. I grip her soft arms and the book falls upon the floor with a thunk. Her head moves and suddenly, there is no peace in her face. The smooth, white arms beneath my hands are chill and lifeless and my Elizabeth is gone, perished. A vision of blood and darkness clouds my mind as I cry for help, hopeless though it is. A sound in the corridor permeates the walls and I turn in horror and fury. Suddenly, inexplicably elsewhere, my sweat drenched head twists and smacks the soft down of my pillow, together with my clenched fist. My eyes crack open to observe the dim luxury of my chamber at night. And my loud breathing continues, although everything else is gone.

The next day, Miss Bennet's health is restored, and the Misses Bennet depart. Although, I am certain that the younger would have imparted news of the strange and tragic events that had taken place while the elder slept, when the two ladies sweep down the great staircase and make their farewells, it is not mentioned. As Miss Elizabeth and I bid one another a courteous goodbye, the winter sun bounces on her clear skin as she curtseys and my neck prickles. I do not feel equal to further conversation. Following our discussion in the library, my subsequent dream, and those long, dark hours as sentinel outside her chamber, the lady has begun to occupy my thoughts on an almost permanent basis. She has bedded down inside my mind. She is like the log in the fire that has "taken" and the heat of her sustains everything else. The blaze is increasingly too large to manage. If my feelings for Miss Elizabeth do not change, despite the inferiority of her connections, I have no honourable course but one. For the moment, if she is safe in her family home at Longbourn, and not a great distance from me, then that is enough.

The affair has somewhat marred the revelry that may otherwise have attended Bingley's settlement in the area. It had been Bingley's intention to host a ball and Miss Bingley was anxious to impress upon me in particular that she was able to organise the same to the very highest standards. Alas, it is not to be. Bingley is adamant that, for six months at least, a house in which a man has been brutally robbed of his life, is not a venue for a party. Miss Bingley perches upon her silk covered chaise and pouts.

The inquest into the man's death takes place four days after the murder in an upstairs room at the King's Head in Meryton. We have been informed in advance that Miss Bingley and Mrs. Hurst will not be called as the testimony of Miss Elizabeth, Bingley, Wilkins, and myself, being the first four persons on the scene, together with a handful of servants, will be enough. Although I am by no means in favour of gentlewomen being interrogated in public, I am discomforted by these arrangements. If poor Miss Elizabeth is to be put through such an ordeal, why should the Netherfield ladies be spared? And, in any case, is it not a confession of ignorance? I know in my bones that they are not being called because there is nothing they might say. There appears to be nothing that anyone can say, and that fact presses upon me.

When the morning comes, Bingley has arranged for an additional carriage to carry Wilkins and the servants who are to give evidence. They each clamber into the conveyance, looking about gingerly, dressed as if for church. Hurst accepts Bingley's invitation to join him in his carriage and climbs into it as though he is attending a racing meet or a night at the opera.

"Are you quite sure you will not join us, Darcy? It looks like rain, man." He glances at the shadowy sky, clouds roiling above our heads.

"It will pass. And Meryton is only two miles. I shall be fine. Gather your thoughts in comfort. I shall see you at the inn."

And with that, I prompt my horse and am away, slightly ahead of the Bingley entourage, the morning air biting my face. It is not that I spurn luxury, for I do not. There is a time and a place for all things, and if others wish to sit at ease while they contemplate the event to come, then so be it. It is not for me. The feeling of movement and chill air on my skin is my best preparation, and I know it. As it is, the rain holds off and the ride is too short.

The market at Meryton has all the indications of a place where an unusual event is about to occur. Bodies jostle about and voices are raised. Stalls are set up selling various wares, plainly in the hope of additional trade. A number of carriages are stationed outside the King's Head, as well as in the archway, and stable boys stand about tending horses and barking instructions to one another.

I give my horse to one such boy, and approaching the low entrance, almost collide with Mr. Bennet escorting his second daughter in the same direction. Behind them, much to my relief, stands their own carriage. I hardly know the limits of peculiarity in the Bennet household, but it is reassuring to see that at least on some occasions, daughters of the household are afforded proper treatment. Between us men, we hint at bows and Miss Elizabeth curtseys, her dark skirts pooling on the dusty ground for a moment. I stand back and allow them to pass before following her through the public bar, down a long, dingy corridor, and up the rickety staircase. We emerge into a room which I suspect is little used. A motley collection of mismatched chairs is lined up in the middle of the room, but there are nowhere near enough room for the crowd which has begun thronging in through the narrow door. Miss Elizabeth looks about from under her bonnet, but her father does not indicate that she should sit, which plainly she should. Instinctively, I move towards the wall, where I intend to stand for the whole proceeding. At length, Miss Elizabeth is seated with Mr. Bennet, Mr. Hurst, Bingley, and a number of others behind her. At the front of the room is a long table and to the side is a small one with a three-legged wooden stall placed behind it. The rabble of the room grows noisy and women bustle in with jugs of ale to roars of appreciation from some. It has never been my misfortune to attend an inquest into a man's death, and I know little what to expect. However, it is plain that the event is a local spectacle and I rather doubt that the vast majority of bodies in the room have anything to add to the matter apart from their own curiosity. The object of that curiosity, of course, is plain to see. I avert my eyes, as does Miss Elizabeth and her father, but there are many here present who have no such scruple. For to the left of the long table, in a darkened alcove, is another table. And upon it, an open coffin with a cloth draped inexpertly over its gruesome contents. It is a requirement that the body be present at the inquest in this way, but that is hardly a comfort. Whilst strange voices gasp and necks crane among those standing, I see the soft curls at the nape of Miss Elizabeth's neck as she looks to her lap. A fresh surge of anger and frustration that she must be here at all floods through my chest.

After some false starts, the coroner, a wide and red-nosed gentleman named Mr. Kettle, barrels into the room, accompanied by a small boy in an ill-fitting frock coat, and commences proceedings. He sits behind the long table, facing the assembled company, and appears to be no more familiar with the order of things that I am. His bloated hand shakes as he holds a sheet of paper and bellows out the names of those who are to speak. Fortunately, Mr. Allwood, who has arrived late, sits beside him and occasionally speaks in his ear, no doubt directing the man aright in some way. In turn, those people make their way to the small table, where they sit in varying states of agitation, and answer questions.

The first witness is one Matthew Smee, a footman at Netherfield, who had seen the dead man twice on the evening in question—first, at about five in the afternoon, whilst attending to some silver in the kitchen. They had exchanged words, although Smee could not recall what they were. Second, he had observed him walking past the outer kitchen door at about eight o'clock, when the family and guests were at dinner. He has no special knowledge of the man and confesses to not really thinking about him at all until it became known that he had expired. When Smee is asked whether the deceased had ever spoken of his home or his family, he raises his eyebrows, shrugs his shoulders, and replies: "I shouldn't say that he ever did, sir. Sorry, sir." The only information of value which appears to emerge from his testimony is that Smee has observed the victim out of doors but close to the house at about eight o'clock. The young man appears altogether pitiful throughout and it is a mercy when he is released and returns to his place standing against the far wall with other servants and bystanders from the village.

He is followed by Wilkins who sits unsteadily on the stall before the assembled company and recounts how he first interviewed and then took on the deceased, who he refers to as Partridge. He had seen him in passing on the day of his death and had nothing further to add. His account of the scene of his discovery is perfectly in accord with my own recollection.

Molly, the maid of all works, follows and in her willingness to talk offers a contrast to the previous two witnesses. A small girl with a shock of curly, black hair peeping out from under a cap and a round, beaming face, she sits on the appointed stall as if she has been born to such things. Having given her name and address to the inquest, she proceeds to comment that Mr. Bingley is a "lovely" master and she cannot think how such an awful crime has happened and she never did trust strange men "what come in off the streets" and it is only to be expected "with the war on." Having been fetched back to the subject by Mr. Kettle, she confirms that on the evening in question she was chopping vegetables for Cook while the deceased and Smee were polishing silver at the servants' table. She confesses quite openly to listening to their chatter while she attended to her own work and concurred with the previous account that the man called Partridge had left the kitchen at about a quarter to five.

"Are you sure about that, Molly?"

"Positive, sir. I followed him."

From my vantage point at the edge of the room, I observe the blanket of heads flicker up at this unexpected admission.

"You followed him? And why ever did you do that?" asks Mr. Kettle, his colour rising to an improbable degree. Beside him, Allwood remains inscrutable.

"Well, I'd finished the vegetables, sir. Cook wasn't about. That Sally was in the kitchen and I've heard all her chatter before. I saw Tom Partridge get up and saunter out, and I thought, 'I'm gonna see where yous is goin'.' So, I put down me knife and I followed 'im out."

"Were you in the habit of following him?"

"I shouldn't say as it was an 'abit, sir. But 'e took me fancy a bit. Not that I'm a light skirt, coz I'm not. You can ask the other girls. I jus' noticed 'im. 'E was tall and a bit fine. 'Ad lovely eyes what looked at you but di'n't see you. I'd tried it on talkin' to 'im a few times, sir, but 'e wasn't bitin'. Never said nothing about himself, which I thought was odd. Most people, you can't stop 'em goin' on, but 'e was like a shut up shop. So, I thought I'd give 'im another go like."

"I see. And what happened?"

"Well, it was an odd thing, sir." She pauses, looking around the room of wide awake expressions and gaping mouths. My own feeling is that young Molly is enjoying her moment as the centre of attention.

"We was walking down the corridor, and he said, 'Not now, Molly. Run along before you're missed.'"

Mr. Kettle began to scratch his pen on the otherwise blank sheet of paper before him, splashing ink on the landlord's table and his own cuff in the process.

"And what did you say?"

"I wasn't jus' gin' to give up. I said 'Give over' or the like. 'I jus' wanna chat.' And he stopped and turned to me there and then, all steady and serious like. And he said, 'Later, Molly.'"

With this, her voice, which has been cracking for some time, breaks entirely and she emits loud, fulsome sobs. This outburst is met by a variety of responses in the room, from expressions of sympathy to cries of "pull yourself together, girl." The boy in the ill-considered frock coat produces a handkerchief on which Molly loudly clears her nose before continuing.

"That was it. 'E turned on his smart heel and was off. Left me standin' there on me tod for a bit. And I'll always remember that, sir. 'Is eyes was so calm and clear, like 'e knew jus' what 'e was about. I wish I'd followed 'im now. Coz I might 'a seen 'oo killed 'im."

"What did you do?"

"I watched him go, sir. He turned left out of the servants' hall and I never saw him no more. I stood there a minute thinking as I should crack the closed up old beggar one day, then I went back to the kitchen."

"Thank you, Molly," replies the coroner through the girl's quiet sobs. "You may step down. Now"—he squints into his eyeglass, studying his list—"Miss Elizabeth Bennet!"

A knot forms in my stomach and pulls tight. Apparently unruffled by this disrespectful command and the inauspicious surroundings, Miss Elizabeth rises gracefully from her seat and takes her place before the room. She moves smoothly, with neither haste nor hesitation, and one might almost have thought her familiar with court rooms, if this tawdry affair could be called such. Her clothing is simple and dark in colour and her winter bonnet folds perfectly about her head, shading her eyes—I hoped from the worst rowdiness of the room. The macabre spectacle to her right, she deliberately avoids observing. Having given her name to the inquest as requested, she places her fine, gloved hands on the edge of the small table and awaits Mr. Kettle's questions with an air of calm expectation.

"What were you doing, miss, at around five o'clock in the afternoon on the day in question?"

The knot tightens and expands. Why is he asking Miss Elizabeth to go back so far? Surely the only relevant account she could give is her discovery of the body at nine. What she was or was not doing in the hours that preceded is her own affair.

"I was attending to my sister, sir."

"Yes. Miss Bennet, who had been taken ill at Netherfield, is that right?"

"Yes."

"And where did you attend to her?"

"In the chamber Miss Bingley had kindly made available for her, sir. It is on the upper floor, two doors to the left of the staircase."

"I see."

"Having checked that my sister was comfortable, I readied myself for dinner with Miss Bingley and her family."

"Did you do that in your sister's chamber?"

My finger nails print crescents on my palm and my chest tenses. Her father should stand and stop this, but he does nothing. His arms and legs are crossed, and he observes his daughter being interrogated on her personal movements with equanimity. The lady herself appears entirely calm and answers the impertinent question with nary a blink.

"No, sir. My own chamber during my stay was adjacent."

"I see. Were they adjoining?"

"No. To enter my own chamber, I came out of my sister's and into the corridor."

"Did you see anyone?"

"Not in the corridor, no."

"What happened then?"

"Before going down the stairs, I checked again on my sister. She was resting. I then proceeded to the saloon to join Miss Bingley and Mrs. Hurst."

"What time was this?"

"It was approximately a quarter to seven."

"And which staircase did you take, Miss Bennet?"

"The main staircase, sir. I then walked across the hall, past the drawing room and into the saloon where I found the rest of the company, sir."

"*They*, being?"

"Miss Bingley, Mr. Bingley, Mr. and Mrs. Hurst. And Mr. Darcy."

She paused, threading her fingers. Did I imagine that emphasis on my name, that deliberation?

"And what followed?"

"Some happy discussion, sir, with refreshments and some music from Mrs. Hurst, who is an accomplished pianist. After a time, I cannot recall how long, but it was not above half an hour, the party dispersed briefly before supper. I believe Miss Bingley required to speak to the servants and others had matters to attend to."

"Did you?"

"No, sir."

"So, what did you do during this interlude?"

"I went to the library, sir. The weather out of doors was cold. And I had started an enjoyable book the previous day."

"Explain to the inquest please, madam, where the library is in relation to the saloon?"

"It is the adjacent room, sir."

"So, you went to the next room. Was that really necessary, Miss Bennet? Could you not simply have read your book in the saloon and awaited the return of your hostess there?"

"It was not strictly necessary, sir. However, I was a guest in the house and anxious not to be an inconvenience. Mrs. Hurst and Miss Bingley had departed the saloon. I felt it only politic for me to do likewise."

"Was there anyone in the library who can verify your presence there?"

"No."

My body aches and I realise that I have been holding my breath throughout this exchange. Nothing so debilitating appears to trouble Miss Elizabeth whose voice remains steady and her countenance calm. To think that she had been alone in the library while I was alone in the saloon troubled me. What could be her reasons for not remaining with me and reading her book? For had we not enjoyed several diverting discussions? Had there not been a closely knitted sympathy in the air between us, almost forming? The rasping diction of the coroner continues, no less rudely.

"I see. And how long were you absent in the library before reconvening?"

"About ten minutes."

Her recall is excellent in the circumstances and I feel the coroner ought to compliment her on it.

"And on your travels about the house, Miss Bennet, did you observe anything peculiar? Were you witness to any person in an unusual place or undertaking an irregular activity?" He peers through his eye-glass and I do not like the man's tone.

"Not that I can remember. On my way out of the saloon, I

observed a couple of servants in the hall, but they did not appear in any way unusual."

"Now, you had supper with the Bingleys, the Hursts, and Mr. Darcy, is that correct?"

"Yes."

"What happened when that meal drew to its close?"

At this question, she pauses but only for a moment. Her almond-shaped eyes flash up, she takes a deep breath, and begins to recount it.

"When Miss Bingley suggested that the ladies separate, I indicated that I would take my leave to briefly visit my sister. I had not seen her for above two hours and was anxious not to leave her for long. Leaving the dining room alone, I turned left and crossed the hall before going down the narrow corridor that is adjacent to the music room. There is a small staircase which leads to the part of the house where my sister was."

"Can you explain to me why you did not use the main staircase which is, on your own evidence, the way that you came down before supper?"

"Yes. The small staircase is by way of a direct route, sir. It is quicker. I was anxious not to appear rude to my hostess who had been very kind and intended to check on my sister and return as soon as may be. I anticipated that my sister would be asleep."

"I see. But you didn't get that far, did you?"

"No. When I turned into the hallway leading to the staircase, I saw something on the floor. I did not realise immediately what I saw, but I knew in my heart that it was not a sight to be welcomed. I hurried towards it. At some point, sir, I saw the man's hand and all the blood, and thereupon his form."

"What did you do?"

I lean forward, impatient for this to end.

"I believe I screamed, sir. The dead man was a fearful sight indeed, and I cried out. It was rapidly evident to me that he was dead."

"And why was that?"

"Enough, sir!" The words lurch from my mouth of their own voli-tion and the whole room turns. Bingley tilts his head, trying to catch my eye, but I avoid it. I am in no mood for pleasantries. Miss Elizabeth moves her eyes from the coroner for the first time in her evidence and rests that warm, gracious, enveloping gaze upon me.

The coroner is not so generous in his expression.

"What is this spectacle? You have something to say, sir?"

Mr. Kettle's colour rises and the buttons on his waistcoat strain as he pushes himself forward. Beside him, Allwood touches his arm and speaks softly.

"I do wonder, Kettle, whether this line of questioning is more appropriate for the physician? In my view, you would not be wrong if you moved Miss Bennet on to the next area of questioning."

The coroner let out an indistinct noise and twitching his bulbous nose, continues on another tack.

"Erm, yes, well. In that case, Miss Bennet, please tell me this. Did you observe any other person in the hall at the time you discovered the deceased?"

"No. There was nobody there. The first person to arrive was Mr. Darcy, quickly followed by Mr. Bingley, and thereafter, Mr. Wilkins."

"How quickly?"

"They appeared seemingly within moments of my having cried out, sir."

I exhale and lean my taught frame against the wooden panel behind me. It is a relief to know that she believes I came to her with all the speed I could muster.

"And finally, Miss Bennet, did you know or recall anything of the dead man?"

"No, sir. I do not believe that I had ever seen him."

"Thank you, Miss Bennet. You may step down."

Such is the relief I experience upon her testimony being complete, I am indifferent to my own commencing. Amid the raucous tumult of the room, my name is called. I take my place, as the others have done before me, and answer the man's questions. Conscious that I may have embarrassed Miss Elizabeth as well as myself by my outburst, I deliberately avoid her eye. That being complete, Bingley is called, and he completes the evidence of those at Netherfield at the time of the discovery.

The evidence of the physician, a Dr. Carmichael, is not without interest. Blessedly, he is the only witness who is required to consider the body laid out within the room. He does so quickly, and it is, quite properly, shrouded again. His account is that when he examined the body at eight o'clock the next morning the man had been dead for between twelve and sixteen hours, which put the time of death between four and eight o'clock the previous evening. This is undoubtedly troubling, for had not Smee and Molly agreed that the victim departed the kitchen at approximately a quarter to five, only to be seen again at about eight? When Miss Elizabeth happened upon him at nine o'clock, he was unquestionably dead. The puzzle of exactly when this man had died plucks a chord in my mind which I cannot hush.

There being no witnesses left to hear, Mr. Kettle rises augustly from his position and accompanied by the attendant boy and Allwood, departs the room. Shortly thereafter, he reappears, crashes a small mallet with unnecessary force upon the table and pronounces his finding: the man, whose name is unknown, has been murdered by person or persons unknown. Mr. Bennet places his hand on his daughter's back as they stand to return home and my heart thumps wildly to see her form disappearing down the narrow staircase. Behind her, the chaos of the room grows, the din of the local populace deafening as they chance a glance at the body of an unknown man. I depart the melee quite despairing of the state of justice and the condition of my own heart.

CHAPTER 4

IN WHICH MR. DARCY STUDIES THE
MILITIA AND FURTHER TRAGEDY OCCURS

*I*n the days that follow, I make myself useful to Bingley, dine with his sisters, and play cards with Hurst. I write to my sister and deal with a number matters of business. My absence from Pemberley cannot go on forever, nor do I wish it to. Nevertheless, some unspoken motive keeps me from returning. With Bingley, I call at Longbourn to enquire after the health of Miss Bennet. We are pleased to learn that she is well, although the secret object of my own visit is not at home. We are told that Miss Elizabeth is out walking. Upon receipt of this information, I rather forget myself.

"Alone?"

The frills of Mrs. Bennet's cap jitter as she turns her head in response. She sits, in state, in her drawing room, surrounded by soft colours and dappled sunlight. The rain of the previous days has passed and been replaced with a sharp, chill freshness. Every inch of me longs to be out of doors.

"Yes, and why should she not, if it is her wish?" she protests, tilting her head to the side, demandingly. I decline to dignify her question with an answer and turn back to the window, my eyes boring into the land beyond the garden. The chatter of Bingley and the Bennet ladies continues, despite my lack of participation.

"And how do you do, sir? I understand that Mr. Allwood has now quit Netherfield, and we are none of us any the wiser as to the murderer's identity? How dreadful! And so unfortunate when you and your sister had only just arrived in the area. Miss Bingley is such a refined lady, so splendidly dressed! It is quite unconscionable that she should have to contend with this awful affair. I said to Mr. Bennet, if it had happened at Longbourn, I should not have survived!"

"Mama..." came Miss Bennet's soft voice. Staring into the icy, bright garden, I sense the young lady leaning in, entreating her mother behind me. I can hardly blame her, for who, being related to Mrs. Bennet, would not wish to quieten her?

"I—" begins Bingley before his voice is overwhelmed by that of Mrs. Bennet.

"Of course, at Longbourn, we know all of the servants. There are no new faces here. No strange men roaming about the place! I cannot be doing with it. But it is a blessing that Mr. Allwood is no longer a daily visitor, as I understood from Mrs. Long that he was. For he is a most off-putting gentleman—"

"Mama..."

"Oh Jane, but he is. I recall his father, and what a gait that man had! I should die rather than have him in my house every day, sniffing about and interfering."

"But Mama, Mr. Allwood is our magistrate. He was assisting Mr. Bingley in obtaining justice for the victim and restoring peace."

"Oh, tish! You have read too many novels, Jane, although fortunately, not as many as Lizzy. I should say that he was wasting time and drinking tea. He has not apprehended the villain, I notice! No, indeed. And when the whole village is speaking of the vagrant who was seen tramping across the fields on the very morning after the murder. My goodness! I am cold to even think of it, Jane. Mark my words that Mr. Allwood is not the clever gentleman you and Lizzy seem to think he is! I'll be bound that it was the work of a travelling lunatic who is far from here by now. What a thought—"

Her voice continued, but I close it out of my mind. My eyes scan the horizon for sight of Miss Elizabeth but find her not. Every movement in the branches, every twitching squirrel on the lawn, I note. My hands ball into fists beside me to hear her own mother suggest that the Netherfield murderer is, as we sit here, abroad in the countryside. Anxious, no doubt, to change the subject of the discourse, Bingley manages to speak as Mrs. Bennet catches her breath.

"Let us pray that is true, Mrs. Bennet, and look forward to happier times. It is a pleasure to learn that Miss Bennet is well."

"Jane? She is in perfect health, Mr. Bingley. It was only a trifling cold, I assure you. My Jane has an excellent constitution. She is never poorly for long. Sit up straight, dear. And what are your plans for Christmas, sir? Do you plan to remain at Netherfield?"

"I do, madam. My relations are in the North and it is too far to travel at this time of the year. I do not have a house in Town. When we travel to London, we reside at the home of Mr. Hurst in Grosvenor Square. But yes, we shall be here in Hertfordshire at Christmas."

"Grosvenor Square? How grand that is! I have been there with my sister Gardiner. I have always observed that Mr. Hurst is very smartly attired. Such a gentleman! Does he have a country estate, as well?"

"Erm, no. No, he does not. My brother Hurst is a town mouse, Mrs. Bennet. He has relations somewhere in the country, I believe, but they are rather distant. There is no estate. His home in London is very convenient though and he makes it available for Miss Bingley and me when our needs require it, which is solicitous. As it happens, Darcy here, also has a house in Grosvenor Square. We were last there, not five weeks ago, before our departure for Netherfield."

I have, despite strenuous efforts, been unable to exclude their combined voices from my head. And, at the mention of my name, I am forced by civility to turn and face the room. Mrs. Bennet's blue eyes fly up in consideration of this new information.

"A house in Town? Very nice, I am sure. Well, I am afraid that I cannot countenance the heat in summer and fog in winter that one must endure in Town. And the smell! No, indeed. And Grosvenor Square, which I walked through once with my sister, I found to be rather too hemmed in. Now, Mr. Bingley, you must be requiring more tea."

~

Later, unable to concentrate on a letter from my steward, I resolve to ride out into the chill air of the afternoon. My body cries out for movement and the notion that I may see her, may have proof that she is safe, beckons me onward. I pass Bingley and Hurst riding the other way along the road to Meryton but give them no more than a nod. The village, a market place, a church, and a number of cottages at the heart of a cluster of smallholdings close to the Great North Road, connecting Town with the North country, has become familiar to me. Through the fields, I gallop as fast as the animal can take me, and in the village, amble gently around the damp square, observing the hurly-burly of its day. Mr. Philips, the solicitor, emerges from his office and greets me before disappearing in the direction of the church. Most unusually, Wilkins emerges from a shop, clutching a package, and then enters the King's Head. I almost take him for a stranger. The cobbled space before me is a crush of activity, full of women clutching baskets and stall holders calling out prices and dogs roaming around for scraps.

I complete my tour of the village without observing Miss Elizabeth and am about to return to Netherfield when I see him.

It is the back of his head that first I observe and the characteristic stretch of the arms he offers when in conversation. An easy motion that speaks of confidence. I would know it anywhere. Feelings of rage and confusion tumble through my mind faster than I can count. I rein in the horse and consider the scene before me. He wears a red coat with a sword that hangs at his side as he converses with a gentleman and a red-haired girl. He has always had a talent for slipping in and appearing unobtrusive in any setting. But he is still George Wickham. A chill washes over me, and the fear in my body hardens. How he has spent the monies I gave him or what he has done, I know not. But he has, by some unlucky chance, come to be here. The afternoon sun glints on the handle of his sword and I have an urgent need to know precisely when George Wickham arrived in the village. Was it before the horrific event at Netherfield, or after? I myself observed the militia moving in—was he among them then?

I am further conjecturing when, a moment later, Mr. Allwood emerges from the tavern together with another military man and makes for the market. They approach Wickham and begin to converse. It is plain in their manner that they have already been introduced. A cold and unforgiving wave of anger rises in me. The magistrate knows nothing. The officers know nothing of Wickham's former life. I know more than I should like. I know of lies and exploitations, wastefulness and greed, misadventures away, and deceptions at home. The men who now surround him do not know, as I do, that he ventured to elope unseen with a fifteen-year-old heiress for his own gain, my own sister. And she, a mere child, whose family had trusted him. I curse the moment that he has re-entered my life, but as I turn my horse to quit the village, he shifts himself, and quite by chance, our eyes meet across the market place. Not wishing to look at him for one moment longer than necessary, I urge the horse forward and make for Netherfield where I resolve to write to my cousin Fitzwilliam immediately. As I move away, I feel a sinking sense of the world moving but not at my bidding.

~

"Charles keeps to his word, Mr. Darcy! He is like a dog who will not let go of his stick and quite refuses permission for me to host any sort of gathering at Netherfield. So, you have him to blame for the narrowness of your current social activities. It is not my doing, I assure you."

Miss Bingley's head lolls back as she says this, revealing a pallid neck and she fixes me with one of her lingering stares. I look out of the carriage window as it creaks from Netherfield. Ordinarily, of course, I would agree with her that an afternoon tea party at the home of a country solicitor would be unlikely to excite me. Today, however is different. I am within Bingley's carriage and bound for the home of Mr. and Mrs. Philips in Meryton, certain of being at last in the presence of Miss Elizabeth Bennet. I have glimpsed her at a distance during my subsequent rides, but I have not called again at Longbourn. Fear that I may be unable to sustain a polite conversation with Mrs. Bennet, combined with worry that by showing my interest too clearly, I may make matters difficult for Miss Elizabeth herself. These considerations have kept me away. It has also been imparted to me, by Bingley, that the Bennets have a relation visiting them and this also counselled against attendance at Longbourn in the days past. I have seen enough new faces recently to last me for some time.

I imagined that the home of Mr. and Mrs. Phillips would be too small to permit inviting even selected members of the militia, but I am mistaken. The small drawing room is studded with red coats and the face of George Wickham assails me the moment I arrive. He observes me and makes an almost imperceptible nod. What would these people think if they knew the truth of him? Bile rising, I am in no mood for the welcoming remarks of Mr. Philips nor the catty commentary Miss Bingley whispers huskily over my shoulder. When I venture to glance back at Wickham, he shifts to reveal that the object of his conversation is none other than Miss Elizabeth. Wearing an attractive green gown I have not seen before, she smiles an easy smile as he jokes. I find myself picturing the hem of that dress sweeping up the stairs at Pemberley. Wickham's eyes fall upon her form as he talks, and I know well enough what he is thinking. It has been my practice to quell my inclination to anger with a pattern of steady breathing and I attempt the same in this moment.

Standing thus, I am approached by a new gentleman, in clericals. As to his identity, I do not have the first clue.

"What an honour is this!" he proclaims and then draws back theatrically before continuing. "I do believe that I am addressing Mr. Fitzwilliam Darcy? Of Pemberley? By my word, sir, what an unexpected favour to have granted me. For I have heard tell of you, sir, from your own aunt, the *superlative* Lady Catherine de Bourgh."

My mind reels to consider what connection this man may have to my esteemed aunt, although I am bound to remark, he appears just the sort of person she is inclined to collect.

"I see. And may I ask your name, sir?"

"I am Mr. William Collins, sir, rector of the very church within Lady Catherine's gift and a grateful recipient of her marvellous condescension. She could hardly be more attentive, Mr. Darcy—but of course, you know that yourself, being family!"

Visions of my aunt, at her most extraordinary appear to me, and I fight the temptation to laugh aloud. However, I know that to dismiss him is beneath me, to say nothing of the fact that I have a duty to Lady Catherine to be civil at the least.

"And how do you find yourself in Meryton, Mr. Collins?"

"I am a guest of relations myself, sir. It has been my great fortune to be visiting with my cousin Mr. Bennet and his family at Longbourn. Mrs. Bennet's table is eminently generous, and my fair cousins have been a particular diversion." He raises his eyebrows and glances in the direction of Miss Elizabeth who continues to chatter with Wickham. Nausea rolls over me. Unsure how else to act, I bow to the peculiar creature and make my way across the room to where Bingley and Miss Bennet are discussing the travelling time to London. Miss Bennet, who has of course been spared the same exchange during dinner at Netherfield on that fateful night, asks me my own opinion. Maybe I am rather sharp: "Too long, Miss Bennet."

Bingley shoots me a reprimanding look and I begin to feel rather abashed. I have become aware that Bingley admires Miss Bennet, and although her wider family is plainly beneath him, they appear also to be beneath her. She presents herself as an amiable, young lady and I am sympathetic to her not only as Miss Elizabeth's favoured sister but as one of the others present on that dreadful night at Netherfield. It occurs to me that had we not been fellow travellers in that tragedy, I might be more wary of her. She is a comely, elegant woman of poor connections and no fortune, who my friend has noticed. In the ordinary course, I may have found myself alarmed. But events have thrown me asunder. As it is, I cannot object to her.

"Miss Bennet, I hope that you are quite recovered?"

"I thank you, Mr. Darcy. I am feeling very well. My health is quite restored. Although, we are all still in shock following the terrible events during my stay at Netherfield. My sister bears it well, but it must be a burden to her, I believe."

With this she looks to Miss Elizabeth, whose discussion with Wickham appears finally to have ended. I curse that she departs that conversation smiling, laughing with enviable ease. Locking eyes with her sister, she moves towards us.

The ladies grasp hands and Miss Elizabeth addresses Bingley. "I feel I must warn you, sir, that our younger sisters"—she pauses and looks towards the two wisps of cream muslin currently gadding about the room and giggling uproariously—"have taken it into their heads that you should hold a ball at Netherfield. They are likely to accost you on the subject, so you would be well advised to get your explanations in order!"

"Thank you, Miss Elizabeth, I shall. But of course, I adore a ball. I should have hosted one already had it not been for—well. In any case, I believe that next summer shall be the time, and I shall invite your sisters to name the date, since they appear so enthusiastic!"

"That shall please them greatly, I am sure."

Her voice has a singing, lilting quality and I cannot stand by without addressing her. I wish for those eyes to be directed at me.

"And what of you, Miss Elizabeth? Have you been walking even in this cold weather?"

She turns to me as I speak, her body rigid and her face tense. She nods by way of greeting but it is a study in decorum.

"Mr. Darcy. I have. I enjoy walking in the fields, as you know. We also walk into Meryton quite frequently. It is an easy distance, and for my sisters, especially diverting since the arrival of the militia. You see that many of our most recent acquaintances are here today. One, in particular, you may recognise."

My eyes do not leave hers, for I know of whom she speaks, and what he looks like. The red coats of the regiment are all about the room. George Wickham is not a worthy man to be among them, but how to tell her that?

"Indeed. You should be careful, Miss Elizabeth, in forming judgements of men whom you have only just become acquainted with."

"Like you, for instance, sir? For I have only just become acquainted with you. It is, what? Four weeks? No more."

"It is above five weeks." In fact, five weeks and six days has elapsed since I first encountered Miss Elizabeth Bennet at the Meryton assembly.

"Well, now you say it, Mr. Darcy, maybe that is enough time to sketch a person's character. Although, I have now had the pleasure of meeting a man who has known you longer. Much longer."

Awareness of Bingley and Miss Bennet standing beside us, confounded, holds me back for a moment before I reply.

"We all have advantages and disadvantages, do we not, Miss Elizabeth? The man of whom you speak has the gift of easy acquaintance. Many have met with him and been immediately impressed. Sometimes they are so impressed that they fancy themselves in sympathy with him. Rarely does it last. He has not the same talent for sustaining the good opinion of others."

"He has been unfortunate to lose yours, sir. For in losing it, has he not lost the advantages he was born with and brought up to expect?" She raises her chin as she speaks, and I exhale in frustration. It is plain that Wickham has lost no time in speaking ill of me and my family. What exactly he has told her, I know not. But his treachery appears to have no end. "In losing his connection to you, his life is changed forever."

"Lizzy—"

On the edge of my vision, the confused face of Miss Bennet steps forward, frowning.

"No, Jane. Mr. Darcy understands me well enough. Did you not once sing the praises of loyalty to hearth and home and family? Surely that loyalty must also extend to those one grows up with?"

"Miss Elizabeth, you take great joy in deliberately misunderstanding me. You credit me with motives I believe you know me not to possess. Is this a game for your own amusement?"

"There is no game, Mr. Darcy. None at all. And no joy either. I have always believed that we should seek to treat with honour those who are socially below us. And where one is lucky enough to have wealth and privilege, one should endeavour to use it for the good of others."

The idea of Wickham, who had been given so much, soliciting her sympathy was maddening, ridiculous. She cannot be so credulous as to simply believe whatever calumny she is told. And yet, I cannot betray my sister and tell her the truth. I wait a moment too long before replying: "I cannot disagree with you."

For the briefest moment, I think I see a chink in her confidence, a look of question that dances across her face, and then is gone. Immediately thereafter the music changes and the two younger Bennet daughters appear, shrieking "Lizzy!" and grasping her arms in the direction of the dancing. In this unsatisfactory manner, she takes her leave of me and is absorbed into the tangle of skirts and courtly movements on the other side of the room. I watch her go and feel quite alone.

I almost fail to notice that the party has increased in number during our exchange. There are now a number of additional soldiers, the rector and his wife and, astonishingly, Mr. Allwood. Allwood slips into the room, nods here and there, accepts a cup of tea and says nothing. After a period, he raises his eyebrows to me. He indicates no desire to converse and therefore I do not seek him out, although it occurs to me that he ought to know about Wickham's true character. I ruminate on how it may be imparted to him. The thought of revealing my sister's story to a stranger brings a bitter taste to my mouth, and I push it away.

The room teems with people and movement and chatter, and a longing to remove myself strikes me. With the new arrivals, the place has become quite unconsciously crowded. Miss Mary Bennet takes to the piano, which makes the atmosphere more stifling still. She has not the talents of her elder sister, and at length, her voice begins to rasp about our heads, accompanied by her ill-timed clunking chords. Miss Elizabeth, who has been discussing with her uncle Philips glances over her shoulder, towards the instrument. I may not be well versed in understanding women, but I know embarrassment when I see it. The lady is frustrated, quite naturally, by the behaviour of her family. And that is why she speaks harshly to me. She is, inevitably, somewhat defensive. That is understandable when one is in the position she finds herself. Thwarted ambition and discontent stir inside me. I need more time with Miss Elizabeth but not time like this.

My feelings of sympathy for her increase when the situation escalates even further. For as her younger sisters hare about the room, and her middle sister exhibits on the pianoforte, Mr. Collins begins to lecture the assembled company. The clergyman, who has not even greeted the lately arrived vicar of the church at Meryton, is standing before a chaise of assorted ladies and a number of gentlemen, holding forth on eminent personages of his acquaintance. He speaks, of course, of Lady Catherine, and of a number of other noble families, living close by her. The man's voice is sufficiently loud that I wonder whether he has obtained some wine from somewhere. Before long, he is engaged with Sir William Lucas in a game of aristocratic top-trumps.

"I am blessed indeed, for Lady Catherine, who demands, nay, enables me to visit her at Rosings Park twice a day, must be the most attentive patroness in all of Kent. Why, even Sir Roderick Black, whom I understand to take a keen interest in the Church, is not so condescending to show that hospitality"—he pauses for a moment tossing his hands up in a gesture of mock humility. He appears to think that he is addressing a public meeting and I feel some sympathy for those sitting before him. Miss Bingley, Hurst, and Mrs. Hurst sit on the chaise, a captive audience as he declaims. I observe Mrs. Hurst squeeze her husband's hand and do not wonder at it. For myself, I turn my back on the performance and stare blankly into the wide, empty market below. The serenade of Miss Mary Bennet, and the speeches of Mr. Collins continue as I close my eyes, unwilling to observe the room a moment longer. Behind me, the babel continues.

"I must say, it is not the first time I have been fortunate. For during my time at Theological College, I had the distinction of being part of a group of students singled out for condescending treatment by the bishop himself!"

"The bishop, eh?"

"Aye, Sir William."

"I am so sorry, did I step on your foot, Mrs. Long? A thousand apologies!"

"Well, our own bishop is not at all a remote figure, is he Lady Lucas? Why, he visited the church here at Meryton only last year."

"My dear Miss Lydia, is that wise?"

"I say, it's awfully close in here, is it not, Miss Lucas? I must find a drink, or I shall faint away!"

"I am pleased to hear it, Sir William, but not surprised for I have heard, in ecclesiastical circles, you understand, that he is a most devoted—oh! Good heavens, I am sorry, madam!"

At that moment, the sound of clattering china combines with the gasps of a number of guests, and I turn to see that my aunt Catherine's cleric has fallen over, sending tea all over the skirts of Mrs. Long, upsetting a plate of biscuits, and emptying the contents of his pockets on the floor. It seems to me that the situation has reached the maximum degree of absurdity.

"Mr. Collins!" wail a number of female voices as Sir William helps the man up from the floor.

And so, it continues. From my position by the window, I venture to exclude the hopeless scene from my mind. When, after a period of stillness, I look back, it is to see Miss Bingley and Mrs. Hurst making as if to depart. I believe Bingley would have happily stayed longer, for he is still in conversation with Miss Bennet. However, upon being impressed by his sisters' desire to return home, he takes his leave. There is some delay caused by Mrs. Hurst being given the wrong cloak, a confusion which she is most affronted by. After some degree of coming and going, the error is corrected; we are ensconced in Bingley's carriage and bound for Netherfield. Notwithstanding the allurements of Miss Elizabeth Bennet, I have never been so happy to leave a place in my life.

~

The next morning's dawn breaks sharp and clear across the great empty eastern sky and I venture out for a ride before breakfast. I have letters to write and a meeting to attend with Bingley. The disappoint-ments of the previous day have replayed themselves in my thoughts throughout the night and left me poorly rested and ill humoured. The face of Elizabeth Bennet is my constant companion and my mind rages against it. I cannot let her own me nor can I forgo her presence. This is the conundrum with which I wrestle constantly. Bingley and Hurst are about their breakfast when I enter the room and Wilkins appears behind me with letters on a silver tray which he proceeds to distribute in silence. I recognise Georgiana's hand immediately and am about to break the seal when the door opens. A footman appears and announces "Mr. Allwood" as the man himself strides into the room without breaking step.

Bingley stands abruptly.

"Mr. Allwood."

"Bingley." He removes his gloves, still breathless from his ride and nods to us in turn. "You will forgive this intrusion, sir, but it cannot be helped. There has been another tragedy in the night. I have come from Longbourn." He pauses and runs his hand across his chin. My body washes over cold and I stand, although I feel unequal to it. Images rage through my mind like cannon balls, none of them welcome. Mr. Allwood looks directly at me, the green of his eyes flashing in the morning sunlight.

"What is it, man?" I bark.

"It is the Reverend Mr. William Collins, Mr. Darcy. He is dead."

"The Bennet's cousin? The clergyman?"

"The same."

I struggle to order this information in my head. He was doubtless a figure of amusement, but he had not appeared ill. If the man suffered from unseen health complaints, then what business was it of the magistrate? I return his stare, questioningly.

"I have sent for a physician from Hertford. But at this stage, I believe he was poisoned."

"Poisoned? Whoever would wish to poison a visiting clergyman?" asks Bingley.

"That is the question, Mr. Bingley. He was a cousin of Mr. Bennet of Longbourn and, had he lived, would have inherited the estate upon Mr. Bennet's death. He had no other ties to the area that I can discern. There was some manner of dispute between Mr. Bennet and Mr. Collins' late father, and so this visit was the man's first visit to the home of his relations. He was a twenty-six-year-old curate, unmarried, and unconnected to any manner of criminality. No doubt we will all have formed certain views of the gentleman at yesterday's gathering." Allwood pauses and turns to look at each of us.

"But the fact remains that William Collins returned to Longbourn after the tea party, retired to his chamber in order to read before supper, and was found dead by a maid a couple of hours later, having failed to appear at Mrs. Bennet's table."

Stunned silence shakes itself out across the room like a winter blanket. For myself, I can think of nothing save Elizabeth. Where was she? And who was keeping her safe?

Bingley strides about noisily.

"What is to be done, sir?"

"Firstly, Mr. Bingley, I intend to confirm the cause of death. Mr. Bennet expects the physician forthwith. However, I would not have called here if I was not reasonably certain. I have questioned all of the family and servants at Longbourn. They are small in number."

A shudder works through me. Was it the idea of Elizabeth being examined for a second time or Mr. Allwood's mention of inadequate arrangements under her parent's roof that made me recoil?

"Fact is, nobody seems to know anything. Mr. Collins returned from the Philips', was observed by a maid to be looking poorly, as she put it to me, and expired. He was, as you gentlemen know, in attendance at the home of Mrs. Philips all afternoon where there was ample provision in the way of food and drink."

"Yes?" enquires Bingley, fiddling with his waistcoat. "And what means that, sir?"

Mr. Allwood turns to my friend and regards him with thinly veiled astonishment. As to Bingley's naivety, I must say, I was in complete agreement with the magistrate.

"It means, Mr. Bingley, that he was poisoned under our very noses!"

CHAPTER 5

IN WHICH MISS ELIZABETH IS SURPRISED AGAIN AND MR. DARCY INVESTIGATES

I waste not a moment. The realities of the situation have come to rest in my mind and the necessity of action is clear to me. Two unnatural deaths in a small pocket of a place such as this in the span of a few weeks speaks louder than any considerations I may otherwise have had. There is absolutely nothing for it. After exchanging words with Bingley and Hurst and having assured Allwood that I am at his service, I saddle my horse and depart Netherfield. Heat and chill, I feel all at once as the animal and I thunder through the now familiar countryside. The air is bone-shaking cold but inside myself, I cannot but note a warming when I think of what must come. My own feelings I have known for some time. I cannot stop, nor do I wish to. The thought of her pulls me on, as well as the knowledge that I may protect her from grievous danger. Was this the inevitable consequence of my affections, or has it been thrust on me, at speed by extraordinary events out of my control? I know not, and it matters not.

The approach to Longbourn is as I had come to expect it. Ice capped branches frame the muddy track, grooved by carriage wheels up to the low, ivy cloaked wall that circles the garden. I deposit my horse with a boy at the front of the house and the front door opens for me as I stride towards it. A young woman in a brown pinafore bobs a curtsy, but I hardly see her. Handing her my hat and coat, I pause. I had thought to request an audience with Mr. Bennet, but the girl leads me through the hall and before opening the drawing room door, looks over her shoulder, pushes open the door, and announces, "Mr. Darcy, miss."

Miss Elizabeth stands, and I realise she is quite alone. I had not expected to see her first, or unattended, but there she was. The irregularity of the household, writ bold, but fortunate too. The winter sun winked through the sash windows, throwing a vivid sort of light on the smooth surface of her skin.

"Forgive me, Miss Elizabeth. I am sorry to hear the news of your cousin. It must have been a great shock to the household. You have my condolences."

"Thank you, Mr. Darcy. I am afraid that you find us in a state of some upheaval. May I offer you some tea?"

"No, thank you."

Her lips part, but she speaks not. Collecting her embroidery and placing it on a small table, she looks about her, and then to me. I begin to pace the room. Sweat beads at the back of my neck. Heat presses against me, unrelenting. I move away from the fire, which is far too large for a room of this size.

"Mr. Darcy, would you like to sit?" she asks hesitantly as she slowly sinks to the chaise. Her frock, she had worn at Netherfield on the day she arrived, and her hair is arranged simply. She looks uncommonly attractive and her dark eyes glint as she tilts her head.

"Miss Elizabeth, you cannot doubt my business here this morning. I had hoped to speak with your father, but perhaps it is as well that things are as they are."

Her eyes widen, and a questioning expression crosses her face.

"My father is with the rector, sir, if you wish me to fetch him. My mama is taken unwell with the shock and my sisters attend her. You find me awaiting the arrival of the physician who is expected from Hertford."

"I see. I do not wish to importune your family, but I am sure you see that this matter cannot be postponed."

"Erm..." Her upturned face looks blankly at me. A silence yawns between us and I find myself simply staring at her in hopefulness.

"You must allow me to tell you how ardently I admire and love you. I have struggled for some time, in vain. But it will not do. The circumstances, which are perilous, do not allow for us to linger. I beg you to relieve my suffering, and your own insecurity, and consent to be my wife."

Having fixed me with a most searching stare, she then blinks and looks away. A further silence follows, no doubt shorter than it feels. I begin to fiddle with my cuffs, a sense of unease rising in me. Although she cannot doubt my feelings, she deserves explanation and analysis that only I can give her. My own voice sounds loud in my ear as I continue.

"The comparative situations of our families, I am well aware of, and I cannot say that I am pleased. But it cannot be helped. It is, what it is, and I accept that it is no fault of yours. The response of my family, I cannot vouch for. It is likely to be unfavourable, and rightly so. Indeed, I would advise myself against a union such as this, if only I could."

I trust this to be sufficient for her understanding. I have been impressed by her intelligence from the very first moment. She is not a woman who requires to be hidden from the truth. Indeed, she has informed me of that herself.

"Nevertheless, my affections are yours and yours alone. Now, with this recent horror, I press you for a speedy marriage in order that I may remove you from Longbourn to a place of greater safety."

Images of her at Pemberley tumble through my mind like falling autumn leaves. Elizabeth alighting the carriage. Elizabeth meeting with Mrs. Reynolds. Elizabeth in the mistresses' chamber. Elizabeth *being* Mrs. Darcy. It is as natural a state of affairs as I can imagine.

"A place of greater safety? Where could be safer than the home of my parents, sir?"

"A house in which a man is murdered, neighbouring an estate in which another man was murdered only weeks before is not safe for you, you must see that."

She lets out a breathy noise and turns from me. Her beautiful face is taut, strained, and in this moment, as hard as flint. But she must appreciate my logic; she simply must.

"It is an unassailable fact. Somebody has acted in this way, and nobody knows who. Nobody knows where the offender is or what his intentions are. Your own mother informs me that you are allowed to walk out alone. I approach the house, unannounced, and there is not even a servant on the door to guard the five young women and their mother within. I have never observed a male servant here who is not a gardener or a stable boy—"

"Mr. Darcy—"

"You are not protected as you should be nor as I would protect you. At Pemberley, I know who is who and what is what and you will be secure there."

"Mr. Darcy. I implore you to stop."

"Stop?"

My chest tightens.

"Stop. I shall not be travelling to Pemberley, now or in the future. I thank you for your offer. But, I am unable to accept it. I am sorry to cause you pain, although I rather think that such as there is will be short-lived."

With that, she stands, and her eyes fix me like arrows.

"That being my response, shall I assume that you no longer wish to see my father? He is rather taken up with events and I have no wish to embarrass you."

Her voice is louder than before and not entirely steady. Is she in shock at her cousin's death? Is it the consequence of upset emotions and family feeling that I am so dismissed? She cannot, surely, be in earnest?

"Embarrass me? Am I not *embarrassed* already, madam? To have made the offer I have made and been so unceremoniously rejected? With so little civility? With no explanation of any sort?"

"If it is an explanation you seek, sir, then you may have it. Although, I rather wonder at your requiring it."

I take a sharp breath and turn to face the window. Her words spin through the air like splinters of ice.

"You have presented your suit in the most ungentlemanly way possible, Mr. Darcy. You chose to tell me that you liked me against your better judgement and that you had struggled against making the offer on the basis of my inferiority. What is that offer, sir, if it is not an insult?"

"Would you have preferred I had not spoken plainly? Is it flattery you seek?"

"No. It is civility I seek but not from you."

Her face reddens, and she turns away. In the middle-distance, a door opens, and footsteps fall. I begin to feel caged, trapped. For all of her ill-treatment of me, I desire nothing but to remove us both from this place and commence matters anew. How can this discussion, which should be straightforward, have spiralled out of control? I am brought back from my thoughts by her voice, clear and steady.

"I seek nothing from you. Even if you had not declared yourself in this peculiar manner, the answer would be the same. You have, from the very first, presented yourself to me as the proudest, most thoughtless of men. My assessment of your character was fixed when I heard Mr. Wickham's account of your dealings with him."

"Mr. Wickham!" I cannot stifle the mirthless laugh her words provoke. Heaven knows what lies he has told her. "And what do you know of Mr. Wickham? Nothing that he has not told you himself."

"I know quite enough, Mr. Darcy. And my sources are my own affair. You have treated him shamefully and care not at the position he finds himself in."

"The position he finds himself in!" I repeat her words, incredulously. I pace the room, but Elizabeth is still as a statue. Her cheeks flush in agitation.

"That is not all. It is in the generalities, not the particulars, you display yourself most accurately. I was struck, almost from the first moment by your arrogance, your conceit, and your selfish distain for the feelings of others. Now, to this list I must add a lack of decency and judgement. To have come here, on such a day as this and pressed your suit to me in this way, I can hardly credit. Did you think that I would be so flattered that I would not listen to the words you spoke? That I would lose myself in the compliment of your offer?"

"Of course not."

"In that case, I cannot account for you at all. I shall not inform my parents of this interview, which I suggest is now at an end. You are the last man in the world whom I could ever be prevailed upon to marry. I pray you now depart before we are discovered."

My mind races to give meaning to her words and my own feelings. I turn to her and catch an expression upon her face I do not recognise. A moment later, it is gone. The truth of her rejection, of her unfavourable view of me, unfolds like a well-drawn map. It is reality, and all else is imagination. I am injured by the wound but determine to remain calm. I am stung and to think of her words stings me further. My chest is tight, and I know in my heart that I should not have come here.

"I shall. And you are right that I should do so. I perfectly comprehend your feelings and shall trouble you no further."

Within a moment, I bow, turn, and quit the room, taking my hat and coat from a quivering girl in the hall and storm from the house. I mount my horse at speed. I do not, cannot, look back. *Never be seen to run from another*, the voice of my father sounds in my jumbled mind. Hearing it, I resolve to trot slowly until reaching the perimeter wall, whereupon I intend to gallop as if my life depends on it. This plan almost complete, I am astonished to see the crouching figure of George Wickham as I round the wall onto the track to Netherfield. He is not wearing his uniform and his face is ghostly white. His circumstances however, are of no interest to me and there is no man in the world whom I wish to see less. Just as I am about to race away, he stands.

"Darcy, I must speak with you—"

"Go to hell."

~

The early morning mist is far from lifted and the earth hard and blanched with frost. The stable boys at Netherfield are surprised when I appear just before dawn. Even so, they saddle my horse without ado and shortly after I am away, galloping to the edge of the estate and beyond. The countryside opens before me, the soft undulations of the South, the vast wakening sky, flecked with pink, the thickets of trees bordering fields, bone-chilling cold. It has none of the drama of Derbyshire, but I admit that it has its own beauty. As I reach the top of Oakham Mount, I rein in the horse. It is a good vantage point, high for the region. From here, one can see the edge of the village, the main artery north and the Longbourn Road snaking through the fields. My eyes study all of those in the murky morning light, wishing it were clearer, but nothing stirs.

I feel in my pocket for the letter and rub it with my thumb, as though the act of touching the parchment should add to its value. It was the work of many hours, and now that it is done and folded within my coat, I am certain that writing it was the best course of action. I have never been a man for lengthy disquisitions where short ones would do. Even as a boy in the school room, I would never waste words nor give too much of my inner self away. And yet, I have spent a sleepless night, writing a letter to Elizabeth Bennet. By candlelight, I procrastinated. However, at length and with no little effort, I achieved it. I managed to write as I seem unable to speak when in her presence. I apologised as best I could. I told her about Wickham. Not a few weeks previously, I would not have dreamed of being so open, so unguarded, still less on paper. But by some means, I have been moved. I have shifted away from my usual place in thought and word and deed, and no one is as astonished as I. The deaths, the spectacle of the inquest, the force of the lady herself have worked upon me. It was my obligation to give her some indication of Wickham's true character, and I did. If it keeps just one young woman safe, then it is better done than left undone. More than that, I realise that I owe Elizabeth an apology for approaching her in the manner that I did.

And now, all that remains, is to give her the letter. To that end, I scan the horizon again. The horse exhales noisily and the leather of the saddle creaks as I move to get a better view. I have almost given up when a moving figure appears on the track below. A simple skirt peeps out at the bottom of a red cloak and atop it, a bonnet, ribbons billowing in the wind. It is Elizabeth, alone. I slow the horse to a walk and wend down the incline to the flat field. My gaze, I keep fixed on her. There are few women of my acquaintance who would venture out alone and at this hour. But then, if Elizabeth did not keep such habits, it would be all the harder for me to speak with her. Having reached the field, but still some distance from her, I pick up speed. She looks up, the thin winter sun bouncing on her countenance. And although I am still some distance away, I rein in the horse and dismount. Elizabeth continues upon her course and I close the gap between us on foot, leading the horse.

As I approach her, she stops. Stepping closer, I bow low to her.

"Mr. Darcy—"

"Miss Elizabeth—" come our simultaneous greetings as our wispy breath mingles in the air. I note how her gloved hands knot before her waist and how her fine eyes flicker around me, as if looking for answers.

"Miss Elizabeth, forgive me. I have been surveying the area for some time in the hope of meeting you."

"Sir, I—"

"Please, madam. Be not afraid that I—it is not my intention to make you uncomfortable."

A ghost of a smile crosses her face.

"In that case, I thank you," she says quietly and makes as if to pass me and continue with her walk. But having her so close, I must complete my task. Reaching into my pocket, I hand her my missive.

"Please would you do me the honour of reading this letter?"

Tentatively, she takes it, turns it over, and studies it before returning her eyes to me.

"I should not."

"Please."

"It is not proper."

"You are perfectly right. It is not proper. And you are within your rights to refuse it. But I ask on this occasion that you do not. I have made many mistakes, Miss Elizabeth, but I have considered this thoroughly. There is nothing in the letter that can cause you harm or distress. Although, it does contain truths which I would impart to you, if you are willing to read them."

Her eyes play between the letter and my face and her half boots shuffle on the icy earth of the track. The smallest smile of resignation appears, not of passion or friendship, and I feel that my heart might break.

"It is written, of course, without expectation of there ever being a reply."

"Of course not. In that case, I shall read it."

She pauses, and my pulse quickens. Her cape-covered shoulders, which have been so tense ease for a moment and I move slightly closer, not wishing to miss any whisper of a change of heart. A blush creeps up her cheek and the wind stirs the dark ringlets that hang below her bonnet. Suddenly, the horse whinnies and the moment shatters. Elizabeth looks away sharply and slots the letter into her pocket with fast moving fingers.

Before I was ready, she says, "Thank you, Mr. Darcy" and departs. As she moves in the direction of the village, I slacken my hold on the horse but remain standing in the place where we spoke, my feet rooted to the ground. Before me, framed by bare branch and bracken, her figure shrinks. As she recedes, she begins to look like a small, red doll climbing the gentle hill and then as she crests the top, she is gone.

Stephenson oversees the loading of my trunks into the carriage and I consider Bingley's library, I anticipate for the last time in a long time, if not forever. I hear her voice in the hollow silence of the oak clad room and it justifies my planned course of action. I told her that I expected no reply, and I do not. I must remove myself from this place, lest she believe me not in earnest. To Bingley and his sisters, I plead my extended absence from Pemberley and the return to Town of my sister. Those were my declared reasons for leaving. It is not an easy decision and I have ruminated on it at length. For all that she has said to me, I wish to remain. For only with me close by, can I rest that she is safe. Her words, however had been piercingly clear. Only the most stony-headed of men could misunderstand them. I credit myself with enough pragmatism to accept what has occurred and make plans to depart.

Miss Bingley has seen her opportunity and implores her brother to remove as well, pleading distress at events and suggesting that the society in Hertfordshire is responsible for the horrors of the past weeks. Bingley, much to his credit, remains implacable. It is his responsibility as an eminent newcomer, wishing to establish himself permanently, to remain in the area in times of strife, not to turn tail and run to London. He has not said it, but I suspect him of not wishing to leave the society of Miss Bennet. His visits to Longbourn have lengthened and become more frequent. It is not ideal, but I would not be the one to discourage it. Indeed, for my own part, I attempt to use this to my advantage. Convinced as I am that Elizabeth would be safer away from Longbourn, I suggest to Bingley to put it in Mrs. Bennet's head that the ladies of the house may be sent away to stay with relations to allow matters to calm. I can only hope that this plan may come to fruition. Through the window, I see the strapping of the trunks and observe the men confirming their stability. Stephenson assays and then exchanges words with the driver before checking the inside of the carriage. My departure is imminent now, and yet I long to stay.

Without warning, the heavy door opens and Allwood, of all men, appears.

"I hear you are off, Darcy?"

His tone, at once enquiring and also challenging, is characteristically cryptic.

"I am, Allwood. I must go home. I wish you good fortune. I can be reached at Grosvenor Square for the next several weeks, possibly longer. And thereafter, at Pemberley."

In response, he grunts and glowers in his customary fashion.

"I see. If there is a trial, you may be needed as a witness."

"If that happens, then of course, I shall be at your service. But I am doubtful, Allwood. What can I be a witness to? What can any of us attest? The fact is that we are no nearer to understanding these events than we were the day they began."

"I will be the judge of that, Darcy. When a crime takes place, almost everyone knows more than they think they do. One day, and soon, stop and think. Sit down at your finely built desk and write down what you know to be true. You shall be surprised at how much more there is. The innocent bystander is the best witness to truth in this world."

I let out a laugh, unwillingly. Elizabeth's rejection of me and the hopelessness of the hunt for the *Meryton Murderer*, as he has become known locally, converge in my head and forms one large stinging, uncontrollable horror.

"Well"—I turn to face him properly—"I should be grateful that you think me innocent."

"You should."

"Do you not believe in the presumption of innocence then, sir?"

"Not really, no. Not in relation to people who are present at not one but two murder scenes in a short space of time. No. I am a suspicious man, Darcy. If I am to credit another with innocence, then I do not do so unthinkingly. I have thought about your own character, and I am content."

"Is that your manner of announcing that you suspect others, sir?"

"It is. I suspect each and every person present in and around Netherfield and at the Philips'. Servants, gentlemen, soldiers, all."

"Gentlemen?" I could not help raising my eyebrows at this.

"Yes. And ladies too, if you like."

"Impossible. I am not being naive or protective. But it is impossible. It is inconsistent with Smee's testimony. He saw the victim during the course of dinner. And we know that nobody left the table prior to Miss Elizabeth."

"Well, there is that. But I try, in the face of significant provocation, to keep an open mind, Darcy. There are many for me to keep my eyes on and I shall miss your company in doing so."

"My company?"

"Yes. You are careful, watchful. Nothing much gets past you, although maybe you have been preoccupied of late." He allows those words to hang in the air like phantoms and then dismisses them with a sweep of his hand as he continues. "The key fact, that currently defeats me, is the identity of the first victim. I am convinced that if that can be established, then the rest shall follow."

"Is that not an impossible task? A nameless man with no home, no family, no history. A man who appears in a place where no soul knows him and then dies. How are you or any man ever to establish who he was?"

Allwood let out a rare laugh. "By my word, Darcy. Men call me cynical. If I were to think as you do, I should never act at all. For what are the frustrations of this life, if not things to be worked on, beaten? You are right that it is a Herculean task. But it is not an impossible one. I know certain facts. Facts that I have, until now, kept to myself."

"Yes?"

"Firstly, some logistical matters. Mr. Philips, the solicitor, visited Netherfield on the morning of the first murder. He had a matter of business to attend and his appearance was expected. However, he was observed driving his phaeton, alone, back towards the house in the late afternoon, sometime before you yourself returned from your daily ride."

He pauses, and his eyes are filled with challenge. The effrontery of the man in making my movements his business is a stark second to assisting him, if it makes *her* life safer now that she has declined to share mine.

"Go on."

"The previous day, a young woman was seen traversing a ploughed field, alone, bound for the house."

"Any description?"

"Dark hair, pale dress, spencer, carrying a bonnet. Running, apparently."

"I think that likely Miss Elizabeth Bennet. She is a keen walker and arrived on foot. I cannot imagine that it is in any respect relevant to your enquiries."

"Neither do I, but I want to eliminate it. You know more than you think. Everyone does."

"And what more do you know, sir?"

"I know that Partridge, I shall call him Partridge for ease, entered Mr. Bingley's employ exactly seven days prior to his death. I know that a man answering to his description alighted from the coach from London in Meryton and stayed for two nights at the inn in the village, prior to this. He paid for his bed and board and he kept to himself. On his second day at the inn, he was observed to write a letter in the public bar and leave with it in his pocket."

"So, he could read and write? Unusual for a man of his background."

"What background? We know almost nothing about him, remember? But, yes, if he was the man whom he presented himself as, it would be out of the ordinary for him to be literate enough to write a lengthy letter."

"Is there any method of discovering to whom the letter was addressed?"

"I wish there were, Darcy. My only hope is that the recipient may write back. The landlord and his family have strict instructions to fetch to me immediately any item of correspondence addressed to any person who is not residing at the inn."

"So, he was a man of some education. Anything else?"

"He had a leather purse in his pocket when he died."

"How much was in it?"

"Nothing. It was empty. I suspect he was robbed."

"Is that likely, Allwood? Why would the thief not have taken the whole purse? Why waste time and risk discovery in removing money from a purse only to give it back to the victim? Particularly one who was either dead or about to be so?"

He stares at me, hard. I feel rather than understand that I am being trained. For what, I know not.

"You may be right, Darcy. If you are, then there must be an alternative explanation for the presence about his person of an empty purse of some quality."

And with that, he produced from his own pocket a small, pale tan purse. In some respects, it is unremarkable, but upon inspection, I come to see that it was rather an odd thing for the man to have been carrying. It is a rounded object, unable to hold much, and slightly worn at the edges. At the opening is a tendril of thin leather pieces wrapped around in a peculiar formation. I recognise it at once; it is how Mrs. Reynolds ties up the spare linen bags in her office. The memory of home renders me suddenly enthusiastic.

"That's a lover's knot."

"It is indeed."

"In fact, do you not think this object altogether rather feminine? I cannot imagine that it was actually his. Our man could have stolen it himself."

"Possibly, Darcy, possibly."

Silence continues for a few moments, but I am not discomforted. I turn the purse over in my hand, studying it. I have never seen one like it. No doubt having spent too long studying the item, Allwood continues as though it is not there.

"During his week of employment, he had one evening off."

"Yes, you said before. He went into the village, if I recall."

"To be more precise, he spent the evening drinking at the inn. Quite liberally, if the bar maid is to be believed. He had coins in his pocket that night, but he was not ill-behaved. He drank. He talked with the serving girl and a handful of officers and other men. He enjoyed the freedoms of his hours away from Netherfield, and then he returned here, alone."

"I see. If I knew anything further of the man's activities, I would relate it to you. But I fear I know nothing. Except, there is one set of circumstances, known only to me and…another, and I have come to the view that you should be aware of them. It may be of no importance, but I have concluded I would be wrong to keep it from you."

"Go on."

"Amongst the officers of the regiment, you shall find one George Wickham. I have no doubt that you have made his acquaintance. He is a man who is known wherever he is. He and I know one another, from childhood. I would never have expected to encounter Wickham here and I have no idea how he came to join the army. He is the son of my late father's steward. He was a favourite of my father's and he and I grew up together in Derbyshire. We played together as boys. He was afforded a number of advantages not in keeping with his station. I do not say that his treatment was wrong or more than he deserved. It did not, for whatever reason, profit him the way that my father intended.

"George Wickham went to the bad. He grew deceptive when amongst his family and mine and dissolute when away. He ran up debts, he mistreated young women, he made enemies, Allwood. When my father died, he had promised Wickham a living in a parish within the gift of my family. I had, by that time, concluded it was quite inconsistent with his way of life and indeed, he was not eager to take it. I paid him the sum of three thousand pounds by way of agreed compensation. He took the money, in place of the position, with alacrity."

Even the act of discussing the man causes a ball in my stomach to grow, but I continue, reasoning that Allwood needs to know.

"I believe I may have mentioned that I have a sister. She is presently sixteen years old. A gentle, sweet girl. And she is an heiress of considerable fortune. George Wickham has been a feature of her home all her life. So, it is not surprising, I suppose, that when he conspired to meet her when she was staying with her companion on the south coast, she trusted him. I was given to understand, later of course, that there were a number of assignations between them. My sister was led to believe herself in love, and to consent to an elopement. At that time, she was but fifteen years old. As it was, and unfortunately for the designs of Mr. Wickham, I arrived unexpectedly. My sister confessed the plan to me. Therefore, the scheme was prevented."

I look him straight in the eye and know I can trust him with this information.

"I tell you this tale, not because I wish it to be known generally, but because I believe it ought to be known by you. You should be aware of the man's character."

Allwood nodded, said "I see," and began to rub his chin.

"You should also know that on the morning after Mr. Collins died at Longbourn, Wickham accosted me, in an agitated state."

"Where?"

"Outside Longbourn."

"What were you doing there, Darcy?"

"I was offering my condolences." The words shot from my mouth quicker than I could consider their veracity. "It was early. I fear that I was in an ill-humour."

He mutters, and I avoid further discussion of that morning. I have revealed my sister's story to an outsider and that is enough. He gives me his card and I promise to write with any further thoughts if they occur to me. We part in peace with a handshake and a nod of the head.

I bid farewell to my host and hostess and to Mr. and Mrs. Hurst, who exclaim at length that I should not desert them. That being done, I descend the stone steps, board the carriage, and am away. Behind me recedes a house and a village in which a great many events have taken place. Leaning back in the leather seat, with the muted greens and browns of the Netherfield lands whipping past the window, I recall her reproofs, one by one. If I cannot rid my mind of those thoughts, I shall simply have to learn to live with them.

PART II
THE UNKNOTTING

CHAPTER 6

IN WHICH MR. DARCY RECEIVES NEWS, AND AN UNEXPECTED ENCOUNTER TAKES PLACE

The door to the breakfast room opens with the softness of a kitten and Georgiana appears, her tiny black dog forming an excitable luster of activity at the hem of her fine skirts.

"Good morning, Brother."

She advances upon me, smiling broadly, and gives me a kiss on the head, which I return. Presently, she selects her breakfast, and, commenting on the brightness of the day, sits down beside me. The sun flooding through the tall windows lights her golden hair and dances on the fine fabric of her dress, seeming to bring both alive. I am reminded for a moment of our late mother and all other thoughts pause.

My sister, her companion, Mrs. Annesley, and I have been at Darcy House for two weeks now, they in my sister's apartment. And although I am wracked with worry as to events in Hertfordshire, now that I am not there to know of them, I am grateful for this time with Georgiana. She has been my constant companion whilst in Town. Being both averse to large gatherings and the trappings of the *ton*, we have employed ourselves much better. We have been to galleries and concerts and walked in Green Park with the winter sunshine on our backs. The weather has been cold but dry and has enabled us to escape the confines of Grosvenor Square for a number of expeditions, not least to Hatchards, where I believe it was my sister's purpose to strip the enterprise of their entire stock. Each morning subsequently, she has appeared at breakfast clutching a different volume and I wonder at her reading speed. If Miss Bingley ever learns of this voracious rate of consumption, we shall never hear the end of it. The idea that Elizabeth, for she is Elizabeth in my mind, would enjoy a trip to Hatchards gives me pause. For a moment that thought sparkles like a star, and then dies as quickly.

Smiling, absently, I return to my plate when my London butler fetches in my post and lays it upon the table without comment. Of the three letters, I fix on the second immediately. The direction is written rather ill and ink blotted on both sides whilst the corner has crinkled in transit. Still, I have a sense that it is from Allwood and I open it first. The man's manner of writing letters is very like his manner of speaking.

Darcy,

I trust this finds you well. News. Since you departed the county, Wickham has deserted the regiment. He was discovered gone from his quarters one week ago and is suspected to be somewhere in London, although there is no evidence for this. I shall be in Town myself next week and would like to meet with you. I intend to present myself at Darcy House on Wednesday 12 inst. I trust this is acceptable. Nothing further. Until then.

Allwood

I place the letter face down beside me. A great many matters roar through my mind. I have more reason to resent George Wickham than any other man I know. All at once, I see his smiling face and the villainous trajectory of his life. How many of his vices have I been witness or party to? Too many. Between Derbyshire and Cambridge, I have seen trusting men robbed by way of credit, young women misled into impropriety, and much else besides. I blamed my own naivety at one time and reprimanded myself that I did not perceive sooner my friend's lack of scruples. Memories flood back to me. Writing cheques to cover the man's debts, attempting to make good the shattered connections he left in his wake. Inevitably, because of how Wickham chooses to live, he can never remain in one place for long. The long arm of human comprehension, to say nothing of the law, always necessitates his turning a new leaf, and moving on to the next set of unsuspecting souls. For this reason, his disappearance from Meryton should come as no surprise to me. But all the same, even for him, it appears hasty. I read Allwood's letter again, tracing my eyes over the ill-formed scratch of the man's hand and then place it face down on the table beside me.

"Is everything alright, Brother?"

"Yes, quite well. Did you sleep well, dear? I heard thunder in the night."

"Quite well. I do not believe that Hawksmoor enjoyed the storm though."

I glance back at the creature, and find him in his usual location, curled beside my sister's skirts, asleep.

"The truth is that I did lie awake for a short time. You will think me awfully silly, but I am so excited about attending Mrs. Protheroe's this week—I could not sleep."

The carriage draws up outside the fine property in Bruton Place. I step out and, surveying the row of stucco-fronted, iron-framed terraces, assist Georgiana and Mrs. Annesley from their own seats to the pavement below. Dusk has slipped in between the day and the night and a gas light shines on Georgiana's happy countenance as she looks up at me from her winter cloak and bonnet. The famous yellow fog of London has descended, but somehow, she permeates it, maybe through sheer force of enthusiasm. Although she is young, I cannot regret the decision to allow her this evening out. She is, after all, with Mrs. Annesley and me, and we are visiting the home of my godmother for an evening of music. It can hardly be more appropriate for her. She squeezes my arm slightly as she takes it and we mount the steps together. Mrs. Annesley, who has been companion to my sister for a year now, stands on the other side of Georgiana, exclaiming with joy at the soft sounds of music that drift through the glass into the darkening street. We three enter the home of Mrs. Protheroe with much expectation of a pleasant evening.

Lavinia Protheroe's lobby reflects taste, thought, and a willingness to spend money that is redolent of the lady herself. In the capacious, candlelit hall, with Protheroes past and present peering down at us like gargoyles, we shed our heavy cloaks and headwear. Georgiana, who I note is wearing her favourite gown, takes my arm once more and we are announced into the drawing room. As the door opens, a number turn towards us, ringlets bouncing and smiles widening, all of them familiar, some of them Fitzwilliams. At the centre, the towering, silk clad figure of our hostess with her familiar shock of red hair, stands and swans towards us.

"Darcy, how lovely."

I bow to her as she turns her attention to my sister.

"My dear Georgiana, how marvellous to see you here. I have been looking forward to this evening all the more since Darcy wrote that you were to come. I am quite thrilled." The lady, who had been a girlhood friend of our mother, touches her hand to Georgiana's arm so lightly that I suspect she barely senses it. "I must say, you are looking quite the young lady, is she not, Darcy?"

I gave no answer, knowing one is not required.

"And Mrs. Annesley, how are you, my dear? I hope well?"

"Yes, thank you, Mrs. Protheroe."

As she beams, the elderly companion's shoulders settle, and a new spark starts in her grey eyes. I recall how Lavinia had specifically requested that her invitation be extended to Mrs. Annesley, despite the fact that my presence would render her attendance unnecessary. It is as typical of our hostess as it is unusual in the generality of the *ton* that she has such a memory for individuals, whatever their station, and will never lose an opportunity to increase their happiness.

The remainder of the room are all friends and family. My cousin

Edward and his wife. The children of Mrs. Protheroe and their spouses, all of whom are known to Georgiana and me. It has been Mrs. Protheroe's practice, since the death of our mother, to keep a watchful eye on us both. When I have been in Town, she has usually called within a few days or sent me a note indicating that she expects to be called upon. On more than one occasion, she has appeared unannounced at Pemberley, having found herself in the region. Her watchful eyes have followed me throughout my life but especially since my father died. I cannot say that I have not benefited from them. Presently, she draws me into a discussion of Napoleon with her son Archibald whom I have not seen for some months.

Thereafter, we sit and Mrs. Protheroe's daughter Susan plays Haydn at the pianoforte. I am sure that Georgiana plays the same piece more beautifully, but nonetheless, I sit back on the chaise and let the music soothe me like warm water. As the young lady stands, there is a polite applause and a number of voices proclaim the loveliness of Miss Protheroe's performance. It is in the short whirl between performances where remarks are exchanged and fresh glasses of sherry are offered from silver trays that the extraordinary takes place.

The polished teak door of the saloon opens swiftly, and Miss Elizabeth Bennet enters the room, quite as if she is supposed to be there. Doubting my own eyes, I blink and sit forward at once. Led by a servant and accompanied by two others unknown to me, she walks with her customary assurance, greeting Mrs. Protheroe faultlessly as she approaches. Happy words are exchanged and in the din of the room, they laugh. I can hardly take the scene in. What madness has my life become? An unconscionable attachment to a woman of poor connections. Not one, but two murders, presently unsolved. My boyhood playmate and sworn nemesis involved, I know not how. My own ill-considered proposal in the wake of tragedy and danger. And now, the sudden appearance of the lady, right at the heart of my own social circle.

It is almost too much to manage. Almost but not entirely. From somewhere within me confusion and self-pity give way to decorum and benevolence. I see before me how it could be. The thought that I have, through no merit of my own, been offered an opportunity to right a wrong reveals itself to me. There is nothing for it. While my sister chatters to Mrs. Annesley and Mrs. Protheroe flutters her Italian fan, I stand and make my way towards the newcomers. I am striding almost too fast as I stop and bow.

Elizabeth's eyes widen, and she takes a sharp breath.

"Mr. Darcy—"

"Miss Elizabeth, it is an unexpected pleasure to see you here."

I fear my words come out too loud but console myself with their unambiguous civility. Beside us, Lavinia Protheroe tilts her head and pauses before speaking at perfect volume.

"Miss Elizabeth—are you already acquainted with Mr. Darcy?"

"I am, Mrs. Protheroe. We met some weeks past, near to my home in Hertfordshire."

A blush rises in her cheeks and then recedes as her chin tilts up towards me.

"Well then I do not need to introduce you, or to promote his gentlemanly qualities, for you are already aware of them."

Elizabeth smiles squarely at her hostess, but as she speaks, she looks straight into my eyes.

"I am indeed, Mrs. Protheroe. Most assuredly. I should though, if I am not to be terribly rude, introduce Mr. Darcy to my aunt and uncle, Mr. and Mrs. Gardiner."

The couple, who are tastefully dressed and appear to be in their middle years, step forward and introductions are exchanged. They live, they inform me, in Cheapside and met Mrs. Protheroe some years before at a concert and have become in the intervening time, firm friends. Lavinia herself nods politely at this account and touches Mrs. Gardiner's arm before complimenting her gown and asking after her children. Mr. Gardiner, it emerges, is fond of shooting and, rather rashly maybe, I invite him to Pemberley during the season. Mrs. Protheroe declares that to do so would be to travel too far, and he had much better shoot her birds in Surrey, for they were closer to home. With this, the couple is ushered to a side table for refreshment as Mrs. Protheroe's butler approaches and speaks to her in a low voice.

In these circumstances, I find myself standing beside Elizabeth Bennet as the music starts on the other side of the room. We both fix our eyes on the figure of Mrs. Protheroe's daughter Mary plucking at her harp while her sister accompanies her on the pianoforte. My own mind can think of nothing save the lady beside me. As the volume of the music increases, she turns to me and speaks gently.

"Mr. Darcy, thank you for your civility to my aunt and uncle. I am much obliged to you for that. It—it was kind."

"It was no more than they deserve, Miss Elizabeth. They seem very agreeable people. And in any event, they are your relations."

"I hope you do not mind my—well. I trust that you are not interrupted in the enjoyment of your evening by my presence here. My aunt did not intimate to me that you were known to Mrs. Protheroe. I think, maybe, she did not know."

"Please be easy, Miss Elizabeth. Mrs. Protheroe was the greatest friend of my late mother. She is my godmother. She has known me, I am rather discomfited to say, since babyhood. But you have met her. The width and breadth of her social circle is a story in itself, and one invariably makes a new acquaintance or two at any gathering of hers. I have not had the pleasure of meeting Mr. and Mrs. Gardiner before, but I am glad to do so now. I am charmed to see you again as well, if I do not go too far in saying so."

She pauses before speaking and I think I may fall into the chasm of silence between us.

"Not at all." A tiny smile accompanies this comment and, small as it is, is enough to give me encouragement. "I—I read your letter, Mr. Darcy. And you may or may not be aware that since you left Hertfordshire, so has George Wickham deserted his duties. It would appear, therefore, that I owe you an apology, for my assumptions in Hertfordshire. I now believe that they were quite wrong. The opportunity to say so, frankly, is very welcome to me."

Heat races through me and my heart quickens.

"And to me, but I shall have none of your apology, Miss Elizabeth. You did nothing wrong." I catch her shining eyes before they turn away. "Are we to be blessed with your own performance later?" I gesture towards the ladies at their instruments, easily imagining Elizabeth seated behind the Broadwood grand.

She laughs at this suggestion. "I do not think it would be fair on the assembled company, Mr. Darcy."

"You know I cannot agree with you there. But if you are not to play, may I—if it is not too much—may I take up your time still further? By introducing you to my sister?"

There. I have said it. I hope it is unambiguously civil. But do I go too far? It is not my wish to make her uneasy or appear to have taken leave of my senses.

"I should be honoured to make her acquaintance."

"Thank you."

So, it is that we are planted, rooted to the thick pile of the Arabian carpet in Lavinia Protheroe's drawing room, listening to the music, standing beside one another like peaceful acquaintances. It is so improbable that it might be a dream. As the piece ends and the light tap of collective clapping begins, I lead Elizabeth to my sister and introduce them.

"Oh, Miss Elizabeth, how fortuitous this is! I am thrilled to meet you as my brother has mentioned you in his letters."

Heat prickles sharply on my neck and I feel excessively warm. It was true that I had mentioned Elizabeth in my letters, although I never expected her to be informed of the same. The lady looks to me, curiously. It was not the moment to say that I had not given Georgiana anything approaching a full account of the shocking events in Meryton. In fact, I had not intimated anything out of the ordinary had occurred. It is not the sort of information that a girl of her years and sensibilities would understand and I would not be the author of her unhappiness at reading about it. My letters have simply recorded the fact that Miss Elizabeth was a great walker and a great reader and had been a guest at Netherfield, for what else should Georgiana need to know?

"Goodness me… Well, Miss Darcy, I have also heard much of you. From your brother, and also from Miss Bingley, who is a great admirer. She told me that you are a most accomplished pianist. Have you been enjoying the music this evening? My aunt and uncle and I rather regretted arriving a little late when we heard the beautiful piece that has just finished..."

"Was it not lovely? Mrs. Annesley and I adored it. Will you sit with us, Miss Bennet?"

"Thank you, I shall."

And with that, she gave me the smallest smile and sat down. The light flickers on the cream of her gown as she sits and her slender shoulders lean back against the silk brocade of the chaise. I linger for a moment, simply admiring the scene before me—and her person. Something in the way she sits, how she folds her hands and holds her shoulders, makes me want to reach out and touch her. A creature of great power is coiling inside me, and she remains its owner. Content that the three ladies are conversing as though they are old acquaintances, and conscious that I am close to thoughts that may be a source of shame to me later, I obtain a drink for myself and stand to the back of the room. A number of my family accost me in conversation, discomforted as they are by silence. I exchange pleasantries with my cousin Edmund and compliment the Protheroe girls on their performance. The chatter of familiar voices and the clink of glasses on polished wooden tables accompanies the soporific melody of the music. I watch how Elizabeth's head bobs towards my sister to speak in her ear and inclines to listen as the movements change. A chestnut curl kisses the nape of her neck and she has a habit of threading and re-threading her fingers together when she concentrates. She wears, I assume her finest gown, which I have never seen before. It is a simple creation in cream silk and fits her form with an almost negligent beauty. This scene appears to me to be as far away from the Hertfordshire of our acquaintance as it is possible to be.

I become aware of Lavinia Protheroe stationed beside me a moment later than I should have.

"So. What have we here?"

She speaks with provocative leisure. Her grey eyes flick towards me and she takes a sip of her sherry, brow arching. "A young gentlewoman, who you apparently are acquainted with, but whom I have never heard of, apart from in passing from her aunt. Now, if it stopped there, it would not be odd at all, of course. The world is full of persons who have met on one, or even two occasions, meeting again, is it not?"

She pauses, employing her trademark Socratic technique. If she were a man, I would have maintained my silence. But Lavinia Protheroe is my godmother and was my mother's best friend. She is in her fifties and I am a guest in her home. She is also, in her own manner, unbearably charming as well as ruthlessly inquisitive. At length, therefore, I answer her questions.

"It is."

"There are even people in the world, I am told, whom I do not know."

"Are you putting this to me as a topic to debate, or as a truth you have adopted?"

"You know I like a debate."

"I do. But there is nothing to debate, as you well know. It is, of course, true that there are not merely some but many people in the world with whom you are unacquainted. You may be the best connected woman in London, but what does that mean?"

In the corner of my vision, I see her smile, playfully. She has a way of drawing me out, and she knows it.

"I do not deny that you possess a sort of social brilliance. Because you do. But you do not know everyone there is to know."

"How very bold you are this evening, Fitzwilliam. What can be the cause I wonder?"

"In any case, knowing and not knowing are relative terms. Just because one knows a person's name, that is not to say that one really knows them, is it? Have you ever thought how many people of your acquaintance are barely more than mysteries in human form? Even if you had Miss Elizabeth Bennet on one of your lists or you had played bridge with her mother or danced with her great cousin at your coming out or some such—you would not really know her. To go back to the matter at hand. It is not at all surprising that a young, unmarried woman from Hertfordshire, who has never spent significant time in Town, should have eluded you."

"No, indeed it is not. But it *is* odd that you know her, while I do not."

"You know I hold you in the highest esteem, Godmother. But you do not travel with me everywhere."

"No indeed. I cannot abide horses, as you know. This is why I must ask questions, Darcy. And you must tell your poor, old godmother the answers and keep her abreast of events. Now—this Miss Elizabeth Bennet"—her eyes turned towards the ladies on the chaise and she flutters her fan enough for both of us—"how did you come to meet her?"

"You would not credit it if I told you."

She raises her eyes and I know that far from deterring her, I have interested the lady even more.

"She was lately a guest at Netherfield. At Charles Bingley's house—"

"Yes, yes. I understand what you refer to, Darcy. I read about it in the news sheets. And of course, I received your letter. Goodness. Was she...present?"

"She was. She discovered the crime, in fact."

That fact sits like an ache in my head. In how many ways have I re-enacted the whole business in my thoughts to avoid that aspect? I could have discovered the body or Bingley or Hurst or one of the servants. If only Elizabeth had not gone to check on her sister, she would never have left Miss Bingley and Mrs. Hurst. She would have been smiling over tea cups in the drawing room when some other unfortunate soul saw what she had seen. Alas, it happened the way it happened, and there is nothing to be done about it.

"Then I am sorry for her. What a ghastly thing to have in one's life, even accidentally. It speaks in her favour that she is here at all."

"It does."

"It also speaks for your regard for her that you tell me this. There are some, Darcy, who would see it as a sort of blot on a girl."

"Nonsense. How can the innocent discovery of a crime whilst one is undertaking a blameless, ordinary task be a blot on anyone's character?"

"Hmm. You may very well say that. The world is an unfair place. It is significant to me that you do not judge her for it. Indeed, you go further."

"How so?"

"Well, as far as I am aware, you agreed to Georgiana being here this evening because almost everyone here is a Fitzwilliam or a Protheroe, and she so loves the music."

"That is correct."

"And yet, within moments of Miss Elizabeth's arrival, you introduce her to your sister. And you have left them to themselves for most of the evening, forming their acquaintance without your presence."

"Should young ladies not occasionally be left in peace to enjoy one another's company, Mrs. Protheroe?"

"Of course, they should, Darcy. But you forget that I have known you and Georgiana all your lives. I saw you watch over her as a baby. I saw you as her brother and lately as her guardian. We have been by ourselves and with family, as well as with a smattering of others here and there over the years. The manner and the extent to which you have sought to protect her has not escaped me. It is not every new acquaintance you would permit, still less encourage, to sit with your sister without the chaperone of your own eyes. And so, I express surprise, nothing more. For now, at any rate."

Having made her point, she ceases moving her fan, clicks it closed in her small hand, and rests her eyes on the ladies before us. We remain, without words, as the musical performance of my cousin Victoria reaches its conclusion. At the usual clatter of polite clapping, our hostess moves towards Georgiana and sits beside her. Before long, peals of laughter are emanating from their direction and it is a great joy to see Elizabeth among the merry. Noticing that both Elizabeth and Mrs. Annesley lacking drinks, I obtain two and walk towards them. They thank me and feeling emboldened, I sit beside Elizabeth, who does not appear to be offended by the action.

"I hope that you are enjoying your visit to Town, Miss Elizabeth?"

"I am. It is most diverting. I am staying with Mr. and Mrs. Gardiner and have been treated to all manner of sights and adventures."

"I am pleased to hear it. Do you stay long?"

"At least four weeks, sir. It is arranged that I shall remain with my aunt and uncle for Christmas and then return to Hertfordshire in January, if the roads are not too incommoded by the weather, that is."

"That is always a danger. Georgiana and I shall be unlikely to return to Derbyshire until the spring now. For many roads in the North become perilous in the winter months. Were it just me, I would brave the elements, but with Georgiana in my keeping, I shall be cautious. I would usually endeavour to be at home at Pemberley for Christmas, but what with the events of the last few weeks, I have been delayed and so shall remain here."

"Well, I am sorry for you, if you would rather be at home. It is one thing to be away from one's home on a welcome break, as I am. It is quite another to be kept away by circumstance when one would sooner be there."

"No, I assure you—"

"Miss Elizabeth?" came the voice of Georgiana, her neck craning somewhat to meet Elizabeth's eyes.

"It would be an honour if you and your aunt would visit with Mrs. Annesley and me, and take tea at Darcy House during your stay in London. If you are not too busy, that is."

"Miss Darcy, that is a very kind invitation. Thank you. I shall be delighted and know that Mrs. Gardiner shall be likewise."

"Oh, good!" Georgiana breaks into a smile and her eyes crease at the edges. "How about tomorrow?"

The matter is settled shortly afterwards with Miss Elizabeth and Mrs. Gardiner expected at Darcy House in the afternoon the next day. My sister, who I have no doubt is aided and abetted by Mrs. Protheroe, is alive at the prospect and as she slips into our carriage at the end of the evening, her tired eyes sparkle. On the other side of the street, the hunched figure of the watchman passes bellowing "one o'clock and all is well" into the night air. As the carriage clicks and rumbles its way through the darkened streets, Georgiana slumps against me and I feel, even in those short minutes between Bruton Place and Grosvenor Square, her breathing becomes steady and her form grows heavy against me. Her sleepiness serves almost to emphasise my wakefulness. For every aspect of my mind and body is alert and alive with the prospect of seeing Elizabeth again.

CHAPTER 7

IN WHICH MR. DARCY RECONNOITERS

The next morning, having risen at dawn, I attend to a good many matters of business before Allwood is announced. He stalks into my study like a man who has lived there all his life and sits by the fire without being invited to do so. I note that he wears the same battered frock coat which he had sported in Hertfordshire, and his hair, if it is possible, looks even less presentable than before. He continues in his habit of looking a man straight in the eyes, unflinchingly, as we speak.

"Allwood, welcome to Darcy House."

At this, he merely grunts.

"I hope that I find you well?"

"You do not find me well, Darcy. A man cannot be well with the unsolved murders of not one but two souls hanging about his neck like a boulder."

"I take it that you have made no further progress then?"

"None whatsoever."

"I am grieved to hear it. What can be done?"

It is an honest enough question, for I know nothing of such things.

"The truth is, that we are at a great disadvantage. And the more time elapses since the crimes were committed, the greater that disadvantage becomes. Time is of the essence. And it is slipping away. If this were France, we could call upon the powers of the professional police but not here."

I smile to think of what my own father or any of my uncles would say to this suggestion.

"No indeed. You would never get that past the Englishman and his liberties."

"Liberties indeed. What does it lead to? I'll tell you. It leads to the enforcement of the law and the safety of the public being entrusted to a rag tag collection of incompetents and chancers. Look at village constables. They are almost never willing occupants of their position —usually and quite reasonably more interested in their regular life than their duties. Magistrates are rarely better."

His eyebrows rise and a rare spark of humour lights his features. He is not, of course, referring to himself.

"I recognise what you say. Fortunately, nothing of this sort has happened near Pemberley, as far as I know, within living memory. But the local constables and unpaid magistrates are, I grant you, only able to deal with lesser crimes. Mr. Bowler, the constable in Lambton, knows what to do with a ne'r do well poacher. I am not sure how he would cope with a murderer, and I little think he would know either."

"That is the problem, Darcy. Even in Town, it is better but not much. Bow Street have their eyes open when they believe it will line their pockets. But in the final analysis, they are paid sleuths, half of them with a criminal history themselves."

"They say it takes one to know one, do they not?"

"They do. But I am not sure that helps us. How many men are there who can connect with the mind of this criminal? Precious few I should imagine."

"Shall you need to involve Bow Street in this?"

"I would prefer not to, but I cannot rule it out. You might think it prideful, but I believe I can find the culprit myself with assistance from right thinking people who were actually present."

His eyes stay me for a moment before he continues.

"I have offered a reward locally for anyone with information. Bingley put it up. He has deep pockets, your friend. I do not like to be having to buy the truth but there it is."

I understand his point but am pleased to hear of Bingley acting thus. Far from shrinking back in the face of tragedy and confusion, the master of Netherfield appears to be growing into his position. He has, at last, begun to show that he is worthy of his fortune, and I am glad of it.

"What brings you to London, sir?"

"What brings any man to London, Darcy? Necessity, of course. I should never volunteer for the place if I did not have to. Dreadful. I will shock you when I say that I rather agree with Mrs. Bennet on the subject of our metropolis." He raises his eyebrows as he says this, and I smile in response.

"I did not know that you had had the pleasure of Mrs. Bennet's views on the subject."

"There is not a man in three counties who does not know Mrs. Bennet's views on just about every subject. Finding people who agree with them is another matter."

"Hmm. So what necessity beckons you here?"

"It is twofold. Firstly, and predominantly, I intend to find George Wickham. He was last seen in his quarters at four o'clock on Wednesday last. A serving girl from the King's Head believes she saw a man answering to his description boarding the post to London about an hour later. And not a known soul has seen the devil since."

"Hmm. Well, if he has any sense, he will go as far as possible and disguise his appearance."

"Yes, but not entirely so, Darcy. You are right, of course, that he has the military authorities on his tail. He would, as he will know, and as I am sure you know, do well to avoid them. I have no doubt that doing that is his primary intention. However, I am not persuaded that he would leave London. We do not know how heavy the coin in his pocket, but he probably does not have that much. It might take him into the country beyond Town, but where then? And how does a man hide in a small place where one is a newcomer? He has no family to speak of. He has no friends who are not simpering women or passing acquaintances. No. I will wager he has not left London. Where better to hide than in a crowd?"

"I see your point."

"But damn it, Darcy, where is the man? And why did he run? He may be bringing death upon himself if he is caught."

"Why do you think he left?"

"Would that I knew. He had debts, it turns out. And he had been misbehaving with the miller's daughter. But that is nothing that could not have been resolved in some manner, surely? I struggle to believe that either could form the motivation for a man to desert the King's service in which he was reportedly doing well. The risk to him appears greater than any discernible benefits. Which does of course, play into the generally accepted view."

"Which is?"

"That he was, is, the murderer, Darcy. Both men. Partridge, or whatever his bloody name was. And Collins."

I exhaled and regard his cynical expression. Saying it aloud makes it no more convincing. George Wickham is a scoundrel and an opportunist. But a murderer? I cannot credit it. Allwood appears to sense my scepticism.

"He had the opportunity. He was present at the Philips' and on the evening of Tom Partridge's death, he was already stationed in Meryton. Anyone could have gained access to Netherfield that night. The place was like a bloody sieve."

"Come now, Allwood. The opportunity of which you speak applies to almost everyone. It certainly applies to me. It applies to so many people. The Philips' had invited half the county. Lord knows, they had invited far more people than they could accommodate. As for Netherfield, if marauding members of the regiment could have walked in, then so could any other resident of the village or beyond. What of motive? Why on earth should George Wickham do such a thing? Of course, we still do not know who Tom Partridge was. But why should

George Wickham have known him? And as for Collins, I know of no connection at all. Wickham was present when Collins was poisoned, but they did not appear to know or speak to one another at all. In fact, that may be an oddity in itself, for Collins was talking to everyone, but I do not recall him talking to Wickham."

I paused, and the motion of my mind seems to slow. The effort of recollection is a physical act, one that challenges me greatly. I trace my mind through the party in Mrs. Philips' home, and scenes dance through my head like a poorly received play. Our arrival, my sighting of Wickham, my brief conversation with Collins, my agonising exchange with Elizabeth, the bustle, the heat, the agitation. I cannot recall any indication that Collins and Wickham knew one another, but of course, I was hardly watching for it. The memory of standing at Mrs. Philips' window, in high dudgeon, as the party continued at my back, returns to me. I am regretful now, for is it not the case that in turning away, I failed to observe the scene that unfolded? What did I miss, and shall I ever know?

"Forgive me, but the more I think about it, the more I see it for the unlikely explanation that it is. I am no romantic when it comes to George Wickham. There are probably few men in the world who hold him in less esteem. But I know the man for what he is. He is a taker of chances, Allwood. Where you and I see a friend, he sees a source of advancement. He never took a step or spoke a word that he did not count in shillings and pence. Now, there he was, with a commission and a source of income and respectability. I know how he will have valued that. He would not have risked it, Allwood. He cheats at cards to win. He does not throw his hand in the air and evacuate the room because the air is a trifle stifling."

"Then why did he leave?"

"The George Wickham I know? There are only two possibilities. Either he has a chance of advancement far beyond that which we credit him. Or, he considers that by staying he is in great danger. Danger far greater than that arising from an unwise association with a miller's daughter and a few debts."

A servant slips into the room with a tray of tea, and I pause. I have known Wickham all my life, and I am certain I am right. The memory of his crouched figure waylaying, beseeching me, gives me no peace.

"Consider what we do know, Allwood."

"Which is?"

"On the morning after Collins died, which was five days before he deserted, Wickham accosted me in a state of some distress. I regret now that I did not speak with him, but at the time, I could not countenance it. Now, it is some years since we have been friends. It is over a year since I broke with him forever. He knows full well that he would get no easy audience from me. He can only have approached me because he was desperate. That suggests that the second of my theories is more likely the correct one. If Wickham believed himself to be in serious danger, mortal danger even, that may account for his having approached me. Otherwise, I cannot comprehend it."

"It is a damned shame you did not hear him out."

This is a reality which I do not require to be stated.

"It is. But like so many things, it is passed, and I cannot bring it back. However, I realise now that I should have stopped for him. The responsibility of not having done so sits heavy on my shoulders. And, not least for that reason, I am at your disposal."

"Thank you." He gives an unsatisfied expression and exhales loudly. "If I am right and the blasted man has not left the city, where could he possibly be?"

"I do not readily know. He has no family to speak of. Both of his parents are long dead, and he has no siblings. I recall talk of an uncle, but I do not believe that he lived in Town or that the relationship was close. I could not even tell you the man's name. Wickham was up at Cambridge and, during the course of his degree, came to London occasionally. Usually for the nefarious reasons of young undergraduates which I am sure I need not detail for you. I know of no lasting ties made in those days. During his younger years, although he had some flimsy connections, he never had the money to be part of the set he aspired to. He was always on the outside looking in. No, George Wickham has no kin to hide him that I know of. The only conceivable connection that occurs to me is Mrs. Younge."

"Mrs. Younge?"

"Yes. A woman I hoped never to speak of again, still less seek out."

A flood of bitterness and regret courses through me, and visions of the unfortunate business appear like cards being laid out on a table.

"Mrs. Younge. I did, of course, check her references, which were perfectly good. Looking back, I realised that I had been told very little of her history and perhaps I was unduly naive. I rather doubt that any account she gave of herself to me, or any former employer, was the full one. In any event, she presented herself to me as a gentle-born, experienced companion and I took her on to be such to my sister. The address from which she wrote to me was in London. I am sure that I shall be able to locate it. It was Mrs. Younge who was with my sister when the unfortunate business with Wickham occurred. It transpired that the lady's association with Wickham was of some duration. I know not how long or *how long before* she had approached me. But she certainly assisted him in his plan to inveigle himself with my sister. The child whom she was employed to protect and accompany, she thrust in the path of danger and exploitation. Even if I can lead you to her, there is no guarantee that she may lead us to Wickham."

"No, but we must try."

I take a deep, noisy breath and stand jerkily before advancing on my papers beyond the desk. It is the work of a few moments to locate the letters of Mrs. Younge. The address she gave was in Chelsea, and Allwood and I resolve to travel there immediately. To that end, I ask that the carriage be brought round and send a message to Georgiana intimating that I was going out but would be back in time for her afternoon guests. The knowledge that Elizabeth Bennet is expected for tea brings a flicker of light to my heart and I am damned if I am going to miss her for either George Wickham or Mrs. Younge. At the same time, the importance of it all towers above me like a storm. This might be the link that solves the puzzle; it might bring safety to Elizabeth's hearth. It might make amends for the bungling manner in which I advanced my suit to her. I have no choice in the matter.

Allwood is given his dusty hat at the front door and we are away. Within the carriage, he speaks little but gazes out of the window in a pensive manner. One has the sense that he does not suffer from any sort of nerves or lack of social confidence. I do not believe there is a man in the world to whom he feels inferior. It is simply that he does not care to speak excessively and therefore does not do so. I ponder, not for the first time, what could possibly have caused a gentleman born in reasonably privileged circumstances to have so committed himself to this particular occupation. With this thought, the carriage clatters along the perimeter of Grosvenor Square, past the green gated garden, and onto Park Street. Alongside us, horses trot, carriages and curricles rattle, and urchins run calling out for charity. I turn away from the window.

"You did not say what your other reason for coming to Town was?"

"Come again, Darcy?"

"You said when you arrived that your reason for visiting was twofold. One reason is Wickham. Who or what else are we looking for?"

"Well, I do not know, truth be told. It is an odd business. You recall Philips, the solicitor?"

"Yes, of course."

"Interesting facts about Mr. Philips. As you know, he came to Netherfield on the day of the murder and was seen returning again in the evening for no known reason. I asked him why he had returned, and his answer gave me no comfort. Having first denied the suggestion, he then admitted it but said that he had mislaid some papers during his meeting with Mr. Bingley's steward. He said that he returned to ask after them and, having had no satisfaction, returned to his own home. The poisoning of Mr. Collins, of course, took place in his house. Now, I learn that in the last three weeks, Philips has made three trips to London. Two of them, he stayed the night."

"What could he possibly be doing?"

"That is the question."

With that, the carriage comes to an abrupt halt in a narrow street. My coachman, James, opens the door, indicating that we are arrived at Riley Street. I emerge and consider the surroundings. The narrow track on which the carriage has stopped is overhung timber-framed buildings and hemmed in on all sides by an̦ of men, women, children, dogs. Even a chicken appears. The carts and nags carrying bags of goodness knows what. The ac. smell of the river courses about us. A man wearing a frock coat and no shirt bellows from a broken window. It is a low manner of place —pitiful, dirty, hard—little short of a rookery. Faces peer at us through the yellow fog. I never attended Mrs. Younge at home in the course of our acquaintance, for she came to Darcy House to be inter-viewed. This turn of events reveals her to be an excellent actress, if not an admirable one, for I never anticipated in all my imaginings that she lived in such a place as this. For a moment, Elizabeth's reproofs come back to me and mingle with the holler of the raucous street. Have I been too willing to accept respectability where it *seemed* to exist? Was I guilty of reading the chapter but not the notes because a person had worn the correct clothing and spoken in the correct way? If that is true, I am guilty indeed, as I have thrown my sister in the way of danger and heartbreak. It is a fault that I must remedy.

With this in mind and steeling myself for the sight of a woman I would rather avoid, we knock upon the low, wooden door. With Allwood at my side and the veritable wail of the street behind us, I hammer on the wood. In short order, it is answered by a young boy holding a broom, his mouth gaping as he looks me up and down, seemingly unable to speak.

"Good morning, young man. Please can you tell me if your mistress is at home? A Mrs. Younge."

He gulps, still not speaking and clasps the broom closer to his thin chest. Then, he blinks and seems to recall his courage. Straightening, and holding the broom out like some manner of staff, he says boldly:

"Oo's askin'?"

I smile at his forwardness and take a card from my breast pocket before placing it in his hands. His eyes study it busily and his young brow furrows. As it did so, I place my foot over the threshold. For having reached this place, I have no intention of being turned out.

Mrs. Younge will recall my name. If you would give her my card, I would be much obliged to you."

He turns the card over and hesitation plays over his features.

"I was gonna say that there's no Mrs. Younge 'ere, sir, but I fancy you wouldn't believe me on that! So, thing is, she's not in presently. Out and about, like. Can I take a message, sir? Won't cost you that dear…"

He looks so hopeful that I can hardly deny him and reach for my pocket, not yet producing anything. It is my intent to keep him talking, for who knows what he may divulge. It is a possibility that I may never be able to find the dreadful Mrs. Younge or anyone who can lead me to Wickham. The promise of finding them, the idea that I might uncover the truth, flickers before my eyes like a barely seen light. I will not give up on it.

"Of course, that does not trouble me." I took the coin in my hand and hold his eyes, watching how they light up at the sight.

"When is the lady expected home?"

"Maybe today, maybe tomorrow."

I place the coin back in my purse.

"Alright, mister! Tomorrow."

I take it out again.

"And I wouldn't call this her 'ome, neither. More a place that she coasts along between jobs, if you know what I mean. She's a governess sort. Tarries around in grand 'ouses, doin' this and that."

His reserve is breaking down; I can almost see it ebbing away.

"I know a little but thank you. I shall come back tomorrow. But maybe you can keep my visit today under your hat, so to speak."

"I'm not wearin' a 'at!" he says smiling.

"You look like a man who can keep a thing to himself when called upon. Do you recall whether your Mrs. Younge has had any visitors recently? I am thinking that she may have received a call from a tall, slim, well-spoken gentleman. Dark hair, square sort of face?"

"Likes the ladies?"

"That's the one."

I placed the coin in his hand.

"'E was 'ere a day or two ago, sir. Come in the night like."

"Thank you." I place another shiny coin with the one already there and he closes his hand, the mental clinking together quietly, solidly.

"I will return tomorrow. Maybe I should take back my card for the moment?" I smile, and he hands it back, absent even a moment of hesitation. I am almost completely sure that he cannot read, but with the best will in the world, he may drop it, or show it to another, who can. I intend to return here, and I do not wish for either Mrs. Younge or Wickham to abscond in the meantime.

"I know I can rely on you to keep this between ourselves. So, thank you...?"

"John."

"Thank you, John."

"Thankin' you, sir!"

I nod and turn back to the carriage, Allwood following me into its dark interior.

"Good god, Darcy. We shall make a Bow Street runner of you yet!"

A smile comes to my face of its own volition. It is a fair joke, gently and harmlessly made, but it gives me pause. I recall a long-ago evening at Rosings, with my aunt, Lady Catherine, proclaiming loudly and at length, how no gentleman should ever work. Even the business of dealing with an estate, she considers somehow beneath the station of the well born. At the time, I had been a trifle irritated by her words but not out of the ordinary way. It is a feature of Lady Catherine's conversation that it is, frankly, ridiculous. But recalling it now, and in my present circumstances, I know that it is wrong. If I can lend aid in a small way, if I can edge Allwood's investigation closer to the truth, than I shall have employed myself well.

Opposite me in the carriage, as we jolt along the uneven road, the magistrate continues.

"Let us hope that some good will come of it. Now. Before I allow you to return to Darcy House, I must thank you with nuncheon at my club."

I start to object, to adopt my habitual reaction of shrugging off the gestures of others, but he stops me.

"No, no. It is the least I can do, man."

And so, we rumble on. I am not averse to the idea of his club. He is a member at Boodles and able to take me as a guest. New sensations are besetting me each day, so what is wrong with one more? I am content to attend provided that it does not mean that I miss Elizabeth at Darcy House, some hours hence. I think in that moment of her dark hair playing about her neck and the sparkle in her eyes when last we spoke.

I am pondering this happy thought, and the carriage is about to emerge from the thicket of buildings, when something outside the window catches Allwood's attention and he speaks, quietly and deliberately.

"Well. What have we here?" He gives a quick, seamless instruction to the driver to stop the carriage and shoots back within, concealing himself as he stares out into the street.

Instinctively, I follow his eyes out of the window. There, amongst the traffic, weaving down the busy road, on foot and looking about himself, is Mr. Philips. He wears a long, somewhat commonplace greatcoat, and his hat looks like that of so many men. He carries a box to his chest. A young girl approaches him, holding her hands out before her, but he, without touch, shoos her away and continues on his course. Allwood speaks once more to the driver and, just as I think we should lose sight of the man, the carriage ambles round and starts out in the same direction, dawdling at a short distance behind.

"Would we not be better off on foot, Allwood?"

"No. All we need is for him to turn about unexpectedly. He should recognise either of us immediately and would know he was being followed."

Followed. The word turns in my mind like a piece of meat past its prime. How am I to justify myself to Elizabeth, or even face her, when I have been party to spying on her relations in this manner? As I fight such demons, my companion continues, unconcerned.

"As it is, we are in a throng and less likely to be noticed. I have traced the man as far as Town three times in three weeks, but I have never established where the devil he goes."

"Is it possible that you are—well, reading too much into this? I mean, any man is entitled to visit the city if he wishes. Philips is a professional man. He may have professional reasons for being here."

"He is a country solicitor, Darcy. I will wager he does not serve a client further than Baldock. London people use London lawyers. Who ever heard of someone in Town requiring the services of a lawyer from Hertfordshire? His practice cannot bring him here and certainly not so frequently. No, there is something awry."

"You know the man, surely? You are his magistrate."

That struck me as being self-evident. The solicitor in any small town is a pillar of the community. A man everyone knows for better or worse and in some way or another. The lowliest would know him for being almost a gentleman. The highest—well, they may look down on him. Maybe more than they should. But everyone knows who he is and what his habits are. He is, in effect, a public person.

"Cannot abide his wife. That has kept me out of his company. Which, I accept, I am paying for now."

He gives me a wry smile, which I well understand. Have I not also paid in heavy coin for an unwillingness to throw myself into that society?

"You must have known him for some time though?"

"Yes, I suppose it is some years. I must admit that I did not exactly mark it in my diary. He is local. If I recall, he is the son of a clerk in a town some miles from Meryton. He came to the town articled to old Mr. Gardiner, who had the practice before him. Got to work. Married his employer's daughter. Took over the practice. Became a familiar, if not overly interesting, local feature. End of story. I cannot say that I have ever given the man two thoughts together. But I certainly would not have had him down as being involved in anything...questionable."

"Yet, here we are."

"Yes. Indeed."

Suddenly, he calls out a command to the driver to stop. The carriage lurches slightly.

"What is it, man?"

"Look."

He adjusts his seat and I move forward, my eyes scanning the frantic scene. Women cackle, children run about, and conveyances of all descriptions jostle before us. It is difficult to concentrate but concentrate I do as the brown-cloaked figure of Mr. Philips rounds on a plain, wooden door, knocks, and is admitted. In a moment, he is absorbed, gone. I look the building up and down, assuming that there would be some indication as to its function, but I observe nothing. A shop front, seemingly shut up. A plain door. Windows above indicating nothing. The neighbouring property appears to house a haberdashery, in which a young girl stitches in the window. My confusion mounts.

"What the devil?"

I looked to Allwood but his features remain inscrutable.

"Where are we? What is the street?"

"You are in Robinson's Row, Darcy. And as you see, it is not known for lawyers."

"That shop looks shut up. Who knows what exists above. Although, what is that? I believe I see a small plaque above the door. Do you see it, Allwood?"

He strains and confirms that he does. It is quite impossible to read at this distance. We are so near and yet so far. The promise of it, the tantalising possibilities of identifying where he has gone sings through my mind. I begin to feel harassed by the idea that I should do more, take action. Allwood sits back in his seat and for the first time in our acquaintance, he looks the age I assume him to be. Fine lines creep across his face and in the dark of the carriage, his wizened body looks tired. What am I here for, if not to assist? Silently, I tilt my hat further forward on my head, pull my greatcoat together, and step forth onto the street. For the short journey, I keep my head down, calculating that no one but the desperate children running about can possibly see my face. I move swiftly and look up only when I reach the door and read on a dirty, and by no means, well-appointed plaque the words: "Lockwood & Potter, Importers". I turn on my heels and return to the carriage, which has been opened in anticipation. As I enter, the carriage moves off. I am none the wiser and neither is

Allwood. As we rattle our way back into the smarter streets and the sunshine begins to rip through the dense fog of the city, a thought occurs to me. I know exactly the man to send.

~

When I arrived back at Darcy House, the door opens, and a servant takes my hat and greatcoat. Conscious that I am somewhat later than planned and not as presentable as I would have liked, I stride without ado in the direction of my chamber. Stevenson appears, as is his want.

"Ah. Stevenson. I have a job for you. But I should like to refresh first."

He keeps pace with me seemingly without effort—a trait which has always appealed to me about him.

"Yes, sir."

"I have been hacking about the city with Allwood, and I should change before seeing company. After that, how to do you fancy an afternoon off? Well, maybe not off exactly. An afternoon out. Do you know Robinson Row at all? Near Chelsea. You will find in the middle what appears to be a disused shop, rather ragged about the edges and it seems, an office above. The plaque on the door reads 'Lockwood & Potter, Importers'. Next door is a haberdashery with a girl who looked to be in want of society in the window. I would like to know, if you are able to discover it, what exactly Lockwood & Porter import, if indeed they import anything."

"Yes, sir."

"And what their connection, if any, is with one Mr. Philips, solicitor, of Meryton. Is that clear enough?"

"It certainly is, sir."

"Good. It goes without saying that you are to be discrete. I do not want Mr. Philips to be aware that people, even people he cannot identify, are asking questions about him. Spend any amount of money you deem necessary in the haberdashery or any of the other local shops. I leave it to your judgement."

"Thank you, sir." The smallest hint of a smile plays across his lips and he reminds me of my cousin Fitzwilliam, who would undoubtedly have made a joke.

"Now. I am feeling somewhat used and not fit for company. I should like to change before I join the ladies in the drawing room. I had in mind that new shirt you discovered for me last week?" I look to him searchingly.

"Of course, sir, but I am afraid that I may be about to disappoint you."

"How so?" Stevenson never disappoints me. He is a valet without equal.

"Miss Darcy, Miss Bennet, Mrs. Gardiner, and Mrs. Annesley have had, according to the servants at any rate, a very pleasant visit together, sir."

"Excellent. And?"

"Well. They are out of doors, Mr. Darcy. They are not here, sir."

"Not here?"

"Walking in Hyde Park, apparently. I could dress you to join them of course."

My body, which has been running at a pace, slows and stops. I have missed her.

"I think that may be seen as a little over zealous."

There is no merit in beating about the bush with Stevenson. He knows matters for what they are, in outline if not in detail. It is one thing to join a gathering in one's own home. To follow a young lady—who has already rejected one's advances—about in a public place, is quite another.

"Possibly. I leave that analysis to my betters, sir."

"I do not know why, Stevenson. You are more equipped than most of them. Maybe I do not quite believe you."

He shrugs and places my dirty coat on an incidental chair, no doubt intending to deal with it later. I sit, and he removes my boots, we each slipping into our old routines, many times repeated. It is an unremarkable end to a day which held such promise. She has been here, and I have missed her, possibly by a matter of moments. But to chase her now may be too much. I take a deep breath and look about the room. The great bed, that had been my father's before me, the portraits on the wall, linking me back in time. The rich landscapes, the blue skies of the past, the old-fashioned gowns of cousins, aunts, unknown ladies. This room and those images are so far from the places I have visited today. And yet, I know that I must do it. I must travel so far into the darkness, in order to discover the light, if I am ever to prove myself worthy of her.

CHAPTER 8

IN WHICH ELIZABETH RELATES NEWS FROM MERYTON

I take the steps two at a time and the door opens for me at exactly the right moment. I am tired and breathless, and handing my hat and riding crop to the footman, I storm into the hall like a ball thrown from a great height. In the previous days, we have called several times at Mrs. Younge's address, only to find it deserted. To that, I have added further unsatisfactory enquiries. I have spent the early part of the morning making a fruitless call to a purveyor of clocks in Southwark, whom Allwood believed may have been associated with Wickham. It is, we discover, a case of mistaken identity and a thorough waste of time. Latterly, I rode back through the streets, downcast. I do not blame Allwood—he could not be working more assiduously. But the cold hard fact is that in three days of trouping around London, we have made no progress.

"Stevenson, where is Miss Darcy?"

"Walking with Mrs. Annesley and Miss Bennet, sir."

"Miss Bennet?"

"Yes sir. Miss Bennet's uncle is said to have business in the area. He brought Miss Bennet here this morning and the ladies departed a short time ago."

"Do you know where they were intending to walk?"

"I believe Hyde Park was mentioned, sir."

"And when did they leave?"

"Not above fifteen minutes, Mr. Darcy. Shall I fetch your blue coat, sir? I fancy it more appropriate."

"Do you indeed? More appropriate for what?"

"A walk in Hyde Park, sir. Miss Darcy specifically intimated to me that, were you to arrive home after they had departed, you should be a welcome addition."

"Welcome?"

"Certainly, sir. In fact Miss Darcy, may have suggested that she expected you." And before I can add anything further, he is gone to fetch the blue coat.

I must own, as I trot into the park atop my horse, that the blue coat is an appropriate choice. The day is a chill one, but it seems to keep none of the usual crowd away. The vivid green of the park is studded with tiny figures in fine clothes and carriages pulled by pristine animals. The season necessitates a good deal of clothing and all of the ladies in sight are bundled in hardy cloaks, thick bonnets of all colours shading their faces. From the top of my horse, I observe them, my eye skating over each lone walker, or loving couple, or cluster of friends, until it rests upon those I seek. Georgiana walks between Elizabeth and Mrs. Annesley, and the light, cold breeze tosses their collective skirts like a great sail. As I approach them from behind, I slow. The sight of their arms linked, of their winter bonnets inclined to one another in confiding chatter, make my heart feel light. I note, not for the first time, the neat, compact nature of her body, the purposeful nature of her walk. In order to avoid thoughts which would necessarily delay my announcing my arrival, I speak.

"Georgiana? Miss Bennet? Mrs. Annesley?"

I alight the horse and walk for the last few moments so as not to alarm them from on high and am met with a chorus of "Brother!" and "Mr. Darcy!" and "Sir!" They express surprise, deplore the coldness of the season, and invite me to join them. With great enthusiasm, I do, and we proceed around the park, a happy foursome together with my horse that I walk to the side. Georgiana announces that she has heard to expect snow soon and is determined to walk in the morning rather than be confined to the house for the whole day.

"How thrilling it shall be though! I have never seen London in the snow, have you, Miss Elizabeth?"

"No, I have not. I am sure it shall be very beautiful. I must tell you that my trips to Town have been few and far between and generally only in clement conditions."

"How wonderful that you should be with us now then. We have snow every year in Derbyshire, do we not, Brother?"

"Yes, yes, we do. But I must say, that like Miss Bennet's family, I would usually avoid travelling in such conditions. And it is rare that I have seen snow covering Hyde Park. I hope that you enjoy the spectacle when it comes, Miss Elizabeth. As it surely will, if this temperature is any guide." I look to the sky which has that leaden, ceiling-like appearance that is a harbinger of snow. When I look back, Elizabeth's eyes are on none but me. "I believe that if it is the case, then it may prolong your stay here."

I hardly notice as Georgiana and Mrs. Annesley slip behind us and the party moves on quite happily.

"It may well, sir. It had been my intention to travel home soon after Christmas. But I am certain that my uncle shall not permit me to travel in the snow. So, I may find myself in Town for longer than planned."

The wind blew a chestnut curl across her face and I felt the curve of her smile in the pit of my stomach. I have misread so much, misdirected myself to such an extent, that I hardly dare to hope.

"I trust you are not too displeased if that is the case. You shall always be welcome at Darcy House. And I daresay that the city has much to offer, even in the cold."

"That is just what I think, Mr. Darcy."

She turns her face to me and there is an archness in her manner and her look. Am I being teased? Feeling bold, I offer her my arm. The feeling of her gloved hand clasping it without hesitation brings a warmth to my face.

"Good."

"In any case, I have sufficient correspondence from Longbourn and Meryton to give me quite the impression of actually being there. My friend Charlotte Lucas writes to me of village life, as does my mama and my sister Jane."

"Are your younger sisters at home?"

"Not all of them. Mary, who is still greatly distressed at our cousin's death stays at Longbourn, where it is planned that Jane shall be a calming influence. Kitty and Lydia are staying with Papa's cousin in Bath. They were unhappy to be away from the regiment, but it was judged to be in their best interests that they enjoy a period of absence from home."

"Quite right. I trust that they are well, and the rest of your family, too."

"Thank you, sir, that is solicitous. They are. I am afraid that talk in the village is still dominated by the dreadful deaths of our cousin and the man at Netherfield. And with Mr. Wickham gone, people speculate further—well, I am sure you can hazard a guess yourself as to what they say."

"I can. But I cannot say that I believe it."

She blinks in the sharp light and smiles, knowingly. Having been speaking so easily, I am shocked to find that a silence has tumbled in between us like an unwelcome visitor. For a moment, I study the sight of her kid half boots peeking out from beneath the hem of her gown on the sandy pathway as she walks. I, and no other man, walk beside her.

"Neither do I, Mr. Darcy. For it seems too easy. And nothing is ever that easy is it?"

I exhale and smile at this observation. She has never said a truer word.

"No. I cannot fault your logic. No, it is not."

"But it is bleak, is it not? People at home are saying that Mr. Allwood is in no position to solve the crime. They are saying that he should take the reward he has raised to Bow Street. Much is speculated about the Netherfield victim, doubtless most, if not all, quite removed from the truth. He is said to be a savage monster; a Bonapartist spy; and all at once in league with the vagrant who was sighted in the village on the day of the murder."

"Indeed? He is generally taken for a villain then?"

"Oh certainly, yes. Do you think he may not have been?"

"I try, Miss Elizabeth, to keep my mind open on the subject. Nothing is known to condemn or praise the man. The only thing that we *do* know is that he misrepresented himself at Netherfield. Now, of course, the explanation for that may be more or less reprehensible. But the fact of the matter is that it was dishonest. I should say that I would be surprised to learn of any link to Napoleon."

The tinkle of her laughter sounds warm and easy and I long to hear more.

"So, would I. As for the rest of the news, it is much as one would expect. Mr. and Mrs. Hurst are said to be in Town, but Miss Bingley remains at Netherfield with her brother and has had Mama, Jane, and Mary to tea, which thrilled them greatly. I believe that they are getting along splendidly, in the circumstances. Maybe better than any of them ever anticipated."

"Good. It is a credit to them that they are. It cannot be easy. Particularly for Mrs. Bennet. It must have been a great shock for such a thing to happen in her home."

"Yes, it was. It has always been my mama's way to seek out drama, Mr. Darcy. She has an eye for a story and dislikes it when life simply travels by in its accustomed manner. But, poor Mama—she has had more drama at her door than ever she anticipated or hoped for. It is very thoughtful of you to observe that."

At that moment, a fine curricle jostles past us, startling my horse. The motion sets the air about us moving and Miss Elizabeth's ringlets play about her face before she wipes them away with her hand. She hardly seems to notice the disturbance but cleaves to my arm, steadfast.

"In any case, there are some bright promises on the horizon. Charlotte Lucas is to marry a gentleman of our acquaintance in the next village, so Mama and Lady Lucas are busying themselves every moment with chatter of lace and wedding voluntaries and the like. And there is a newcomer in Meryton, a Mrs. Clairmont, who has been a welcome distraction for their minds."

"Oh?" I would have thought that Meryton had seen enough new faces to last for the remainder of the century.

"Yes, indeed. She is a young widow who has taken a house in the village, close to Mr. and Mrs. Philips. I am told that she wears a veil and has a fine cloak and gloves with Chantilly lace. Not that she is very often seen for Mama reports that she stays much within her doors and is difficult to tempt into society, for all that society may be interested."

"How very observant. Perhaps Mrs. Bennet should volunteer her services to Mr. Allwood?"

"Yes, maybe she should! She does notice things, sir. About how people are dressed and how they seem. Or rather, how they wish to seem to others. I cannot say, for all her efforts, and those of Mrs. Phillips and Lady Lucas, that any frank information about Mrs. Clairmont has yet been established. She is a lady in her middle twenties, I am told. Presentable and diminutive in appearance. Her husband died last year, leaving her without other relations. She keeps a serving girl and a small, unremarkable carriage."

"It sounds odd, does it not?"

"Does it?"

"Yes, certainly it does. Why has this lady settled in the area, and why at this time? Is anything known of her people or where she comes from? Does she have any friends or relations in Hertfordshire?"

"Not that I can divine, Mr. Darcy."

"Well, then I call that very unusual."

We continue in companionable silence, the biting wind at our backs, the affectionate nothings of Mrs. Annesley chatting to Georgiana on the air behind us. Elizabeth's report of yet another new resident at Meryton troubles me and I make a note to discuss it with Allwood as soon as may be. Could it be an accident of fortune? Must it be connected? I thought of the vagrant in the village, the marauding Mr. Philips, the deserting soldier, the leather purse with the lover's knot, and the whole strange, swirling chaos. I do not know the answer. Beside me, Elizabeth walks in perfect step, and that is a pleasure to be thankful for.

"Brother, how this walk has flown past us," cries Georgiana from behind as we approach Cumberland Gate.

"We came in the carriage. Shall you ride alongside?"

I nod to James, who has observed the party returning and opens the carriage for the ladies.

"I shall. After you are returned to Darcy House, I am afraid that I have some business to attend, but I shall certainly take you home. I hope that Miss Elizabeth has been invited to remain for as long as it is convenient for her?"

"Oh yes, of course. I should have Miss Elizabeth to stay for the Season if I could, but I rather think her family would miss her. It is lovely that we have become such friends in this short time." She giggles, and I have the impression of her bubbling over. Not a few short months ago she had been too shy to engage in any sort of conversation with anyone outside of our family.

"That is a great compliment to me, Miss Darcy. But you may rue it if it happened. For have my own parents not sent me away to stay with relations?"

The ladies laugh at this quip. And although I could not ever imagine sending her any distance away from me if I had her in my keeping, I laugh too.

"In fact, I believe that my uncle intends to collect me this afternoon."

I hand Mrs. Annesley and Georgiana into the carriage, the step slippery with cold and James proffers them blankets for the short journey back to Grosvenor Square. Turning to Elizabeth, my mind races as I offer her my hand to assist her.

"Miss Elizabeth, I should like very much to see Mr. Gardiner. I have a matter of business that I must attend to directly we are returned to Darcy House. I am afraid that it will take me out of the house, but I shall do my very best to return as soon as possible. And I...well..."

"Yes, Mr. Darcy?"

"I...hope to see him...and you...before your departure back to Cheapside."

"So, do I, sir"—her words almost too quiet to hear as her hand slips from mine.

CHAPTER 9

IN WHICH MR. DARCY MAKES A DISCOVERY

Since the weather is so much improved, Brother, I think I may suggest to Miss Elizabeth that we visit Hatchards this morning. Do you think she shall like to go?"

"Yes. Miss Elizabeth is a great reader. What a splendid idea."

I place my tea cup down in its saucer and consider my sister beaming back at me. A coating of snow, followed by the inevitable treacherous thaw, had kept the ladies inside for two weeks, much to their displeasure. Yesterday, as the winter sun melted the last of the ice, Georgiana sent a note to Cheapside inviting Elizabeth. I am anxious that her family should understand that I take every care of her, and so when she sent back a note to my sister saying that she would be delighted, I sent my own carriage with a maid to accompany her. If all proceeds as planned, they should be on their way as we sit here. In the meantime, I read the news sheet in quiet anticipation while my sister and Mrs. Annesley sew. Before long, the hush is broken by a servant announcing that the carriage has arrived, and Miss Elizabeth is presently alighting outside the front door. With this, my sister and I move to greet her in the hall. The sight of her in the arch of the doorway in her winter cloak and bonnet gives me great joy. It occurs to me that in the intervening se'nnight, I have not merely been frustrated at our enforced absence, I have missed her. Georgiana comes forth with words of welcome.

"Come in, Miss Elizabeth, come in to the warm! Did you see very much snow still on the ground on your way here?"

"Scarcely any. It is gone, and I am happy for it. It is all the better, for I am not one to be housebound!"

"No, indeed. Mrs. Annesley and I have been quite desperate to get out. I have had an idea for our morning. What do you think to a trip to Hatchards? It is only a short ride away and such a wonderful collection. I could stay in there for hours. I shall not, of course, unless you wish to. I went there with Fitzwilliam just some weeks ago, when he was first returned from Hertfordshire, and we had a wonderful time." Elizabeth hands her thick cloak to a servant as my sister says this and the lady's eyes flash up towards me. I think I see a tiny smile grace her features. It warms me. Could it be that all is not quite lost, after all?

"It is quite the best book shop in London. I am sure that you shall find a book to your tastes. Brother, shall you join us?"

"I would be delighted. But I wonder whether you will allow Miss Elizabeth to sit down before departing? She has, after all, only just arrived."

I challenge my sister in what I hope is a joking manner, but I mean it. In Georgiana's new-found confidence and excitement at having her friend visit, she has quite forgotten the young lady's comfort. Elizabeth smiles merrily.

"Thank you, Mr. Darcy. But I am quite alright. If Miss Darcy wishes to depart directly, I am ready for the fray."

As it is, we all retire to the music room for tea and for Georgiana to write a list of titles she wishes to enquire after. Our guest tells tales of her young cousins enjoying the snow in Cheapside and when I recall building snowmen in the grounds at Pemberley as a boy, she smiles a smile that reaches her eyes. For a moment, I feel as though we are alone.

Having determined that we should depart for Hatchards without further delay, the party is in the hall, readying to leave, when there is a knock on the front door. My surprise is only increased when a footman opens the door to reveal a boy standing on the top step. My eyes fall on the slight figure, standing not quite straight, the red hair, the agitated expression. It takes me but a moment to recall the young man from our meeting at the home of Mrs. Younge and although I am pleased that he has approached me, presumably with some form of information, I can only curse at his timing.

The footman, who is plainly confused, speaks at the same time as the boy himself.

"Yes? What on earth?! This is a gentlema—"

"Beggin' your pardon, sir, I knows Mr. Darcy there!"

There is a moment of silence which I break.

"Yes, it is quite alright. This young man has been helping me with a matter of business. He is quite right to come here, and I suspect that he did not know how to find the other door. Maybe Betsy can escort him down to the kitchens and see that he has some soup. I shall be along directly."

"Yes, sir," came the reply, although I fancy that all the servants present believe me to have taken leave of my senses.

At this unexpected turn, the ladies have halted their conversation and are presently collected in a corner of the hall, clutching their bonnets, and no doubt wondering who this astonishing visitor may be.

"I must apologise, but I must, erm, attend to an urgent matter of business. I trust that you ladies will enjoy Hatchards without me."

"That is a shame, Brother."

She smiles brightly as she speaks, but beside her, Elizabeth appears crestfallen. An idea races through me, almost faster that I can fix words to it. Can Elizabeth possibly think that I am contriving to escape her company? Nothing could be farther from the truth, but how can I say as much in front of my sister and her companion? I recall what she had said about a possible return to Hertfordshire and know that I must brave my own pride and make my position clear. I choose my words carefully.

"It is a great shame. I was looking forward to it. I assure you that I do not leave you by choice. Erm. I wonder, Georgiana, do we have any particular plans for dinner this evening?"

"Yes, Brother. Mr. and Mrs. Hurst are here to dine at your invitation. I am surprised that you have forgotten."

Slipping her fine gloves on, she turns to Elizabeth and continues.

"Mr. and Mrs. Hurst are our neighbours on the other side of the square. Mrs. Hurst is Miss Bingley's sister. She and her husband spend so much time in Town, they are almost always here when we are, is that not so, Brother? Come to that, I cannot quite say where they live when they are not in Town. They are much in keeping with Mr. Bingley of course and—"

Elizabeth is smiling, waiting for her moment to break into the flow of Georgiana's words.

"Yes, I have met Mr. and Mrs. Hurst. In Hertfordshire. Mrs. Hurst is a very fine pianist, is she not?"

"Yes, she is. That is a real quality to her. She and I can talk about music. I rather like that, especially when she is on her own."

A shock of obvious gladness breaks over my sister and I fancy her relieved to speak openly.

"Fitzwilliam. I have an idea. Why should we not invite Miss Elizabeth and Mr. and Mrs. Gardiner to join us as well. I am sure that Mrs. Gibbon shall not be daunted. She loves dinner parties. And Elizabeth has already been introduced to the Hursts. It shall be such a happy reunion!"

A flicker of humour sweeps across Elizabeth's countenance which I cannot but share.

"That is an excellent idea, Georgiana, if Miss Elizabeth and her aunt and uncle have no fixed engagements. Nothing would give me greater pleasure than to see them at Darcy House for dinner this evening."

The moment the words escape my lips, I wonder whether I have gone too far? It is my purpose to make myself clear to the lady, not embarrass her beyond all measure—and my sister and her companion into the bargain.

121

"Thank you, Mr. Darcy. I can speak for Mr. and Mrs. Gardiner. I am quite sure we shall be thrilled to come."

She blushes as she smiles and with that I leave them to their book shopping. Not having the time to consider this development, I allow it to sit in a corner of my mind while I walk swiftly through the house, down into the servants' hall in search of my adolescent visitor. As I enter the kitchen unannounced, a footman with his feet up on the long table jumps to stand and a maid mopping the floor fairly shrieks in surprise.

"Mr. Darcy!"

"Sir! Good heavens—"

"Please, be easy. All of you."

The lad, who had also stood, is in the middle of the table, surrounded by others, enjoying a bowl of soup and a great hunk of bread. He pushes it aside and moves away from his chair.

"No, no. Please do finish. Edith, when my visitor has had his fill, please would you show him to my study?"

"Certainly, sir."

She bobs a confused curtsey and looks upon the boy with thinly veiled astonishment as I sweep out of the room. In the oak-panelled space of my study, I ruminate alone. Allwood, I know has returned to Hertfordshire, although I reason that I can send an express and have a message with him in a matter of hours. He, I have no doubt, will lose no time if the matter demands it. The material point is the boy's information, whatever that may be. I might have asked him to step up here immediately, but I saw the relish with which he devoured Mrs. Gibbon's soup and could not quite do it. I am just on the verge of losing patience when a light knock comes at the door, and Edith appears with the boy behind her.

"Thank you, Edith. Please come in, young man, and sit down over here."

I stand, gesturing to a comfortable chair by the fire, which he gingerly takes, looking about him all the time.

"Now. Thank you for your visit, John."

"It is my real name, sir. Honest."

"I believe you. Now. The last time you and I met, you told me that Mrs. Younge had gone away from Town unexpectedly, do you recall that?"

"Yes. Of course."

"I have called at her house a couple of times since then but found nobody there. What has happened since last we met?"

"Well, sir, nothing much for all o'last week. I was fair cursin' coz it's not like 'er to go away like that on so little notice and I knows you was lookin' for information like. So, I was right put out. But then, yesterday, she comes back. Wearin' exactly the dress she 'ad on when she left. Carryin' a bag she was, 'n' you'd reckon they was the Crown jewels inside!"

"I see. Did she have anyone with her?"

"That's the thing, Mr. Darcy. 'E was wiv 'er. You know, the gent you was enquirin' about."

"Do you know his name? What does she call him?"

"She calls him George. I reckon she's a bit sweet on 'im. But he's much younger than the likes of 'er! Anyways, she rushes 'im in. An' she rushes 'im out. They hadn't been in the house upwards of an hour than she's changed 'er togs and loaded things into 'er bag and is only outside gettin' in an old phaeton."

"What time was this, John?"

"About eventide, sir. Anyways, I tried to hear what she said to the driver, really, I did, but there was so much noise in the street. I just couldn't do it. And I thought. Mr. Darcy'll do me in if I lose 'em. So, I did the only thing I could, sir."

"What was that?"

"I jumped it."

"You did what?"

"Jumped it. 'Opped on the back."

I picture this event and am horrified. To be hanging from the back of a moving carriage in the middle of a London street as dark gathered seems to me to be a remarkably dangerous undertaking for a young boy. But since, he is here to tell the tale, I assume that he has not been injured in so doing.

"Went on for miles it did! I knew we was goin' north, but 'part from that, I couldn't tell you where I was. All the while it was gettin' darker. I thought as I should never get 'ome! So, there we was, jogglin' through the streets over bumps and gawd knows what. When we stopped, I slipped off like and hid behind a wall what was nearby. I spied the pair of 'em gettin' out. Laughin' they was."

"Where were you, John?"

"I didn't rightly know, but I sniffed about and it turns out was up in Pentonville. Miles away, it is! Right near the small pox 'ospital, sir. They swans up to a big, blue door, some cove opens it, and in they go. Now, this 'ouse is right opposite the 'ospital, yer can't miss it. I hung about for a bit, watching the windows, thinkin' as they might come out again, but nothin'. I was startin' to a'wonder how I was gonna get back to Riley Street, but I didn't want to leave, sir. I knew you'd like to have information as to what happened to Mrs. Y. I was about to give up the ghost, when blow me down, but the door opens, and out she comes, alone. Wanders downs the steps, as calm as you like, not carryin' the bag she 'ad when she went in. Gets in the phaeton, what's been a'waitin' all the while, and away she goes."

"I see. The man didn't come out with her?"

"No, sir. I stayed and watched for a while. Not a peep from him. I saw him go in and he didn't come out. I couldn't hang about all night, sir, lest I was missed like."

"No. of course not. Quite right. How did you get home?"

"I wheedled a lift on the back of a cab. Spotted an old cove waitin' for his master. He looked like my old dad, so I just asked him straight and my luck was in. Jump up 'e said."

I cleared my throat.

"Good. Well. I am pleased about that." I reach into my pocket and plant a guinea in the boy's hand. He grins widely and squeezes it in his small hand.

"I take it that Mrs. Younge is now back in Riley Street."

"Certainly is, sir. And a right ol' devil she is!"

~

I lost no time in acting upon this information. Having given instructions that John should be given a basket from the kitchen to take home and sent an express to Allwood, I saddle my horse and make for Pentonville. It is true that as one moves north, the city changes character. The buildings jostle in on one another, the whole place appearing more haphazard. These rickety homes and shops are a far cry from Mayfair, but in these past weeks, I have grown used to new sights and it does not trouble me excessively. Had my late honoured father or grandfather ever travelled to such places? I know not, but the discomfort I might have experienced previously in thinking that I am departing from their way of living does not concern me.

The truth is that I think only of the prospect of finding George Wickham and establishing what he knows. All being well, Allwood would receive my message in a matter of hours. However even if he rode for London immediately and did not break the journey as he should, there is no hope of his arrival before nightfall. This is a disadvantage because, of course, he is the more experienced man and he knows the case better than any other. However, as I click through the streets atop my horse, thinking of the interview to come, I am glad to be alone. Before long and after not many miles, the forbidding sight of the small pox hospital appears. Nearby, a green, like a patch of ill-used fabric, stands in the shadow of a church from which people come and go and an elderly man outside the public house sings sonorously. I glance at my pocket watch and find that it is a quarter to four in the afternoon. The house with the blue door, I find easily enough for John has given me excellent directions. It is an unremarkable sort of a place, neither rich nor poor, with neat brickwork and a clean step. There is nothing there to announce anything in particular and in that it is surely well selected as a hiding place. Whoever would think that a fugitive, possibly a dangerous one, has concealed himself here? No doubt the post boy and the girl who cleans the grate come and go, quite unaware that they are keeping company with a wanted man. As I raise my hand to the plain door knocker, it occurs to me that I know almost nothing of what lies within.

After a moment, the door is opened to me by a small woman in a grey pinafore. I announce that I am here to see Mr. Wickham and that he knows me of old. I have my foot in the door, even as she looks me up and down with unabashed suspicion. After a moment of appraisal, she lets out an amorphous grunting sound and beckons me along a darkened hall and into a lightly furnished receiving room. Left alone with the threadbare chaise and spindly legged table, I begin to pace. The window offers a clear view onto the street and it is from there that I turn when I hear the door opening behind me.

"Darcy. How nice to see you."

He strolls into the room as though nothing unusual has occurred, wearing a distinctly civilian coat over his ordinary clothes. An expression of strain flickers across his face, and I see it.

"Wickham."

I do not bow or hold out my hand. Such formalities are neither necessary nor desirable. As it is, he indicates that I should sit and then follows suit.

"I thought you should never come. Here I have been in this lovely house"—he pauses, looks above him, and sniggers. He waves his hands in a manner indicative of nerves—"sitting about, twiddling my thumbs and thinking, 'When is my old friend Darcy going to call?' What does a bosom pal have to do to be found in this hard, old world? I tried throwing myself on your mercy, but you were not interested. Do you recall? I wonder what you were doing at Longbourn that morning? My word, whatever it was, you had a face like thunder!"

He pauses, inclining his head. What he forgets, in all his swagger and bravado, is that I know him. And I know that empty vessels make the most noise.

"How's the family, Darcy? Well, I hope. I see that the fragrant Mrs. Protheroe still makes the gossip pages. What a woman she is! Card parties here and supper parties there. Wish I was invited but maybe that wouldn't be quite the thing just at the moment. Are you in Town for the winter? Yes, of course, there is likely too much snow to return to Pemberley now. What a shame for you. I expect you would rather not be here."

He stops like a wheel losing its momentum on uneven ground and a silence settles in between us. I am not afraid of it and for a moment, simply sit, considering him.

"Have you finished, George?"

To this question, he fidgets but speaks not.

"Because, I rather think that it would be a better use of our time to discuss the matter at hand. That means, that it is for me to ask questions, not answer them. I managed to find you. It was not easy and as you know, I am not accustomed to pursuing others, particularly those who do not wish to be discovered. However, I managed it. I know not how many others are looking and I cannot say how far behind me they are. I suggest that although this house is a present solution, it is not a lasting one. They will come, George. And soon. Time is pressing against you."

His ashen, pale face nods slowly. "I do not disagree with you."

"Now. Coming to the point. I was surprised to find you in Hertfordshire. It seemed to me that you had prospered or certainly found a path in life. You had a commission. You appeared to be getting on, as your father would have put it. I did not see anything in your demeanour to indicate unhappiness or dissatisfaction. It turned out that shortly after your regiment arrived, a man was murdered at Netherfield. But that had nothing, on appearances, to do with you. Unlike the rest of the village, you did not appear at the inquest. In fact, there was nothing to suggest to me that there was any connection between you and that event. Thereafter, you go along charmingly. You attend social gatherings. You are seen in the market place in your red coat and give every indication of enjoying yourself. You are present at a party at which, it later appears, a man is poisoned. But you were far from the only person there. Almost the whole town was present, including myself. Again, I have no reason to think that you are connected to these events at all. The next I know, you are begging an audience from me, outside the home of a local family where a guest of that family has been murdered. I do not accede to this because I have reasons for not wishing to talk to you. However, I regret it. Because the next news that reaches me is that you have run away. Have deserted your regiment, gone without a trace. You have spoiled your own chances, George. It will not surprise you to learn that the manner of your departure has led to the widespread assumption that you are a double murderer. At the very least, you are a deserter. You may get away with it. On the other hand, you may face imprisonment, transportation, or even death. So, my question is"—he shifts loudly in his chair, presenting me with his side profile. George Wickham will do anything to appear nonchalant—"what spooked you?"

"How gratifying it is that you assume I am not guilty, Darcy. I am much obliged to you."

"Answer the question."

He shifts in his seat again and barely looks at me as he reaches into his pocket and withdraws a small, round object. His eyes linger on it as he turns it about in his hand, stroking it with some care. Wordlessly, he places it in my outstretched hand. There, in my own palm, sits a miniature of a young woman. A delicate and not unattractive face, framed by light hair, dressed à la mode, sits against a rose-tinted background. It is finely painted, reverently done. A tiny necklace is visible against the girl's skin and her gown, which is also fashionable, is a pale blue. I have seen miniatures of this sort many times. Holding this unknown face in my own hand and studying it like a piece of evidence causes an odd feeling in the pit of my stomach. For is this not an image of somebody's daughter, somebody's sister, somebody's wife? Squinting, I cannot quite judge whether she is old enough to be a wife.

"I feel better, just giving the damned thing to you."

"Who is the woman?"

"I do not bloody know. It was given to me. By a man I met in a public house in Meryton."

"The King's Head?"

"The very same. Lovely serving girl. At any rate. I was in there, meaning no ill. And I made the acquaintance of a young man. He worked at Netherfield but was on his evening off. He appeared to be having a jolly time, but he was doing no harm. So, I drank with him, Darcy. Exchanged views on this and that. Commented on the state of the local populace, the weather, the promise of future fortune." He laughs but it is an empty, joyless sound.

"Did he give you his name?"

"He gave me the same name, I later learned that he had given others. And it wasn't his true one. He introduced himself to me as Tom Partridge. We talked and drank. He got himself pretty merry towards the end, I can tell you. The hour was late. I had started to think about the necessity for me to return to the mess. My new friend, showed no signs of stopping though. It was just as I was about to make my excuses and take my leave when he produced that."

He glares at the miniature in my hand as though it is a source of poison. "Pushed it across the table and said have a look at that. I looked, I couldn't help it. Now, I wish I hadn't. He told me that that picture was worth a pretty penny. Said there were people who would pay to keep it under wraps, but he knew better. Said he was playing a game for high stakes but he would win, see if he didn't. His only problem he said was that he was playing a lone game against a scoundrel. Said if something happened to him, he wouldn't want the miniature falling into the wrong hands, so he hit upon the idea of giving it to me."

"Giving it to you?"

"He planted it in my hand as surely as I planted it in yours. Said if anything happened to him, I should keep it safe and take it to High-western Manor in Harking, County of Shropshire."

I nod, committing the address to memory, tucking it away like a calling card.

"What happened then?"

"I thanked him for an enjoyable evening, put the cursed object in my pocket, and bid him farewell. We agreed that we would meet again in the same place one week later. I was a bit intrigued, Darcy. You know I like a story; I like a good conversation with someone who is up to something interesting. But it was late. He was drunk. I was fatigued. The evening had run its course and I simply returned to my fellow soldiers."

I remain perfectly still as his fidgeting grows. To see him squirming before me, he looks like a child of ten.

"The news that a man had died at Netherfield reached the regiment quickly, of course. By nuncheon the next day, there was not a man who did not know. I was not alarmed until I heard the man's name. Then, I can tell you fairly, I started to worry."

"Why did you not come forward with the miniature? You could have told Mr. Allwood about your meeting with the dead man and handed the thing over."

"Oh, Darcy, really. I am not one for mixing with magistrates, you know that. Also, I may have been pushing the limitations of my liberties by staying out so late that night. I was anxious not to offend my commanding officers. So, I decided that the better part of valour was silence."

Incredulity threatens to break through my countenance and I know it. Limitations of his liberties, be damned. George Wickham had sniffed the promise of a pecuniary reward, and he had sat on vital evidence for that reason and no other.

"Problem was that I was in a bit of a fix. He had told me that the picture was valuable but not to whom. I supposed that to most men, it was just a pretty picture. But to at least one man, it was worth killing for. I guessed that a man who was willing to kill for the bloody thing would certainly be willing to pay for it. Trick was working out who."

He crosses and uncrosses his legs, and turning, leans towards me. I want to laugh. For had George Wickham and I not known each other all our lives? How he could think I would be swayed by his little tricks of persuasion, I know not. Having moved into position, he continues.

"Then, if would you credit it, along came the Reverend Mr. William Collins. A more ridiculous spectacle you would be hard pressed to find, but he was alert in his own way. He liked meeting new people, Darcy. Like me, he was a newcomer and an outsider. He enjoyed telling me about his patroness when I met him at Longbourn. It was a source of amusement to me to hear the old bag praised so. My memory of Lady Catherine from childhood is not charitable."

"Tell me about your more recent memories, Wickham."

"Well, I met the Reverend Collins and he was what our dear Mrs. Reynolds would call a chatterbox. He talked for I know not how long on almost any subject. If we were in a Greek tragedy, he would have been the bloody chorus. I saw how people rolled their eyes when he appeared and how he had no discernible shame about propelling himself into any social situation. And an idea occurred to me. I still had the miniature, burning in my pocket, you might say. And I wanted to discover who it really belonged to—even to find someone who recognised the lady would be a start. So, I hatched a plan."

He pauses, looking down at his hands, which are not entirely still. I fight to keep my countenance and allow him to speak. But knowing the man, I can guess the "plan", as he calls it. A wave of nausea rises up in me as he speaks.

"I showed the miniature to the late reverend. Of course, he was full of compliments for it. What a fine, young beauty and what a refined countenance and so on. I am sure you can guess, Darcy. You know, I found him to be an impressionable gentleman. A few reminiscences of Lady Catherine arriving at Pemberley in her fine carriage, of her cele-brated virtues, and he was frankly smitten. I had formed the idea that he was a remarkably stupid man. In any case, I told him that I had found the miniature and was anxious to return it to its owner. But I did not know to whom it belonged and was concerned that some unscrupulous person might simply claim it was theirs when it was not. It was, after all a fine object, and who could say that one of the neighbourhood would not see a chance when it presented itself?"

I resist the urge to snort. I want the whole of his story and knowing the truth in order that I may use it for good is less important than expressing my views. My mind's eye sees Elizabeth and she is like an anchor pulling me back to my purpose.

"Go on."

"So, I gave the miniature to Collins for the duration of the Philips' party. For who would be better for establishing its owner's identity than a clergyman? Here, I said to him, was the whole of Meryton society. Gadding about the drawing room, looking their best, laughing their loudest. Here was the opportunity we needed. If a way could be found to produce the object—both Collins and I could keep a watch for recognition."

"Did you give him any clue of the connection between this image and the first murder?"

"No, I did not."

His voice is quiet, but apart from that, I detect no real remorse or even recognition that he had led the man to his death.

"And what did you discover?"

"Nothing." His voice breaks slightly as he looks down. "Collins played his part, ambling about the room boring people half to death, showing the miniature here and there. I observed him displaying it to both Mr. Philips and Kitty Bennet and a number of others. I was unable to see their reactions. At the time, I was enjoying a discussion with Miss Elizabeth Bennet—time which I cannot now consider to have been wasted. In any event, they were certainly not the only people Collins showed the miniature to. Upon departing, some hours later and when many of the more illustrious guests had left, Collins gave me back the infuriating object and said that he had discovered nothing of its origins. We agreed that it had been a worthwhile attempt and parted amicably. I returned to my barracks. The next morning, early, the man was reported dead. I confess, I panicked."

"I remember."

"After I saw you, I loitered in the village for a time before returning and hearing from my fellow officers that William Collins had been proclaimed murdered. I waited for a short time, Darcy. I tried to think matters through sensibly, but there was no sense in it. Whoever killed Collins must know my part!"

"Must they? I think that a rash assumption, Wickham, and one which may ultimately get you killed."

I do not want to discuss his fate but feel obliged. What would happen to this man, I cannot say. Allwood is looking for him, to say nothing of his superiors in the army. Where were they now? Circling around Mrs. Younge as I had done, following up leads, talking with serving girls and boot boys and wastrels for morsels of information. He only needs to be seen once and he is done for. George Wickham's remaining days as a free man are numbered and he surely knows it. I turn the miniature over in my hand, regarding its polished back and well-made hinge. It is small and solid and ought, by rights, to be admired in some family's cabinet, not paraded among strangers in this way. Do I imagine it, or is the size perfect for the small purse with the lover's knot found on Partridge's body? I believe it is. I always thought it rather too small for holding coin and maybe this is the reason why.

"Do I have your assurance, that you have told me everything you know of this matter? Every last detail."

"Upon my word."

"Forgive me, but that is not known for its value."

"There is nothing I know which I have not told you, Darcy. You have every last inch of information I have. I swear it."

I stare at him, hard. He shifts in his seat, but I know he is telling the truth. Why would he lie? He has told me his tale without a shred of regret, except for the position he finds himself in. His life has been a web of wrongdoing and this chapter, surely the worst. Yes, worse, even than Ramsgate. If the army finds him, then his punishment will be no more than he deserves for having exploited an idiotic young man and unintentionally caused his death. It pains me to conclude so, but it is the case.

"Does anyone else know I am here?"

"No, but they will. I sent an express to Allwood as soon as I discovered the address. He will be in London, I imagine, in a matter of hours. It cannot be much more. I expect him to travel first to Darcy House and then here. He cannot be kept away for long nor should he be. You do not deserve that from me, George. You acknowledge that, surely?"

He nods. An awkwardness fills the sparse room which, save for the creaking of poor quality furniture, is silent. I stand, longing to be out of his company and he follows my lead, accompanying me to the door as though I am an ordinary caller bringing gossip and everyday invitations to tea. We bid one another a polite farewell and as I stride down the shallow steps and mount my horse, I do not turn back. I surmise that I shall never see him again. And although I have been wrong about many things, I feel sure I am correct about that.

CHAPTER 10

IN WHICH ANOTHER DINNER TAKES PLACE AND MR. DARCY ALMOST REMEMBERS

*B*rother! Thank goodness you are home. I have been worried out of my wits."

I burst through the double doors into the drawing room. My progress from Pentonville to Darcy House, from horse to chamber, and thence to the saloon where Georgiana awaits our guests, was so swift as to pass in the blink of an eye. The truth is that my mind is utterly full and racing to plan what should next take place. I expect Allwood to appear at any moment. Rather less alarmingly, we are expecting the Hursts and the Gardiners with Elizabeth to dinner. I do not have to wait long, for shortly after my own arrival that lady, together with her uncle and aunt, are announced. Mr. and Mrs. Gardiner are all agreeableness, of course, and make the customary expressions of thanks and admiration that are so enhancing of Georgiana's confidence. I am grateful to them indeed.

But when my eyes fix on her, I know we have reached a moment for action. Her simple gown pleats on the Chinese carpet as she curtseys. That complete, she pulls up to her full height and her almond-shaped eyes return my attention. Elizabeth stands in the drawing room at Darcy House as though it is her home and I know if there is any justice at all, then it shall be. I cannot let her go a second time. Considering these thoughts, we greet one another in a common enough manner and she indicates to me that she had thoroughly enjoyed her earlier trip to Hatchards. Needless to say, I immediately begin imagining us there together, and then force myself to return to the moment at hand.

I was about to address her further when my plans are put asunder by the entrance into the room of Mr. and Mrs. Hurst. Enthusiastic greetings are exchanged, gowns remarked upon, relations asked after, and all is well. Louisa, whom I have come to understand is more polite in the absence of her sister, is particularly attentive to Elizabeth, although I wonder at her reasons. No sooner has the lady arrived than she is fussing, asking after her sisters, and taking far more of an interest in her than ever she did in Hertfordshire. Standing beside Louisa Hurst's fluttering fan and enthusiastic enquiries, Elizabeth remains the same as ever. They appear to be laughing and getting along famously. Anxious not to neglect them, I address Mr. and Mrs. Gardiner who sip at small glasses of punch whilst answering my questions about their children. Although it commences as a matter of duty, I soon find that the conversation of my guests is its own reward.

"I should thank you, Mrs. Gardiner, for having had your niece to stay in Town these weeks. For she has become such a firm friend of my own sister. I rather wonder how Miss Darcy should have passed the time without her."

"It is always a pleasure to have Elizabeth. I cannot say that she is as easy as her sister Jane nor as fawning as her mama. Ever since she was a little girl, she has required conversation and to get out in the world and look upon new things. That, I suppose, Mr. Darcy, is why she has always been my particular favourite."

"Now, now, my dear"—Mr. Gardiner weighs in, cautiously—"did we not once agree that the first rule as a parent is that one may not be permitted favourites? Must not that also apply to the duties of uncles and aunts?"

"Well, yes Mr. Gardiner. But my view of that rule is that it goes to what one expresses rather than what one really feels. We all of us favour some people and not others. Even amongst those we love, we harbour preferences. I should never indicate my view, least of all to Elizabeth herself. And yet it exists and that is that. I am not averse to Mr. Darcy being aware of it, provided of course, that he knows how to keep a secret."

Her eyes quite twinkle as she says this.

"You may depend on me, Mrs. Gardiner. As to what you say, I cannot say that I am surprised."

"Who could be, Mr. Darcy? And it is all the more true when one considers the dreadful event at Netherfield. To have discovered such a scene and borne it so valiantly—that is our Elizabeth, through and through. It is … well—I hardly know how to describe it…"

"Strength of character?"

"Yes, Mr. Darcy, you have the right of it. Exactly so."

"Are you in the habit of hosting your Bennet nieces, Mrs. Gardiner? I imagine that they enjoy a visit to Town as much as you enjoy their society?"

"I cannot deny it. They are a few years older than our own children, and we have such affection for them. Lydia and Kitty, in particular, enjoy the shopping and dear Mary makes a tour of nearby churches whenever she is with us. She remarks that the city churches are so different from country ones, and I believe that she is right. But I should not give you a wrong impression. They come but rarely. It is well above a year since my sister Bennet last brought the girls, and the time before that must have been two years. So, our visitors are not as frequent as you may think."

"Oh? Some of my family have their own homes in London. But those who do not, pay any number of visits to Darcy House. My immediate family is just my sister and me, Mrs. Gardiner. Mrs. Protheroe, whom you know, is my godmother and prides herself on knowing every person in the home counties and beyond. Georgiana and I have any number of cousins and various more distant relations. So often there is a dress fitting or a meeting with business associates that necessitates a trip to London, and thence a visit here."

"How gratifying for you, Mr. Darcy."

Mr. Gardiner laughs at his wife's words, seeming to understand that I do not always find this state of affairs to be a pleasure. Nevertheless, his wife continues. "No, I am in earnest. For losing everyday contact with one's own family, even the more distant ones, is a great sadness. I should enjoy seeing more of mine, even if that did involve some exploitation on their parts!"

"I shall keep that in mind, Mrs. Gardiner. I have no doubt it is wise counsel. In any event—you surprise me. Do not Mr. Bennet and Mr. Philips occasionally find themselves in London?"

"Some of my husband's more distant family live in London; we see them, of course, which is a great mercy. But our brothers Bennet and Philips—I am sorry to say that they are rarely here. Indeed, I do not believe that we have seen our brother Philips these two years together! His practice in Meryton is such as to keep the poor man very occupied indeed." I blink and try not to show my unease at this revelation. Mr. Phillips' visits to Town are as much a mystery to his own family as anyone, it would seem.

While we have been talking, the sound of good-natured conversation and laughter has risen about me. Even Hurst guffaws at some joke. Servants move about soundlessly, adding candles, and the orange light throws shadows on the heavy velvet curtains. The colour of the room shifts to a glow and the warmth that I feel only increases when Elizabeth appears and takes her aunt's arm.

Our conversation continues happily until Georgiana pulls Mr. and Mrs. Gardiner away, announcing that she has a book to show them. This seems an odd thing for her to say, but leaving me alone with Elizabeth as it does, I do not regret it.

"Now, sir. Your secret is out."

"Secret? If I may speak boldly, Miss Bennet, and risk your calling me out, I have no secrets from you."

"Well, you may very well say that. But I have just had it from your sister that you have been receiving calls from none other than Mr. Allwood. And further, that the two of you together have been undertaking all manner of expeditions—she knows not where."

"What indiscretion in a sister! I had no idea she had such skills as a spy. And within my own house, too."

"I should say, of course, that she has no notion at all of who Mr. Allwood is. She merely told me the name she had heard from the servants and she had gleaned, too, that he travelled from Hertfordshire."

"That is something, I suppose. Since I have told her very little of what happened in Hertfordshire, it would surprise me if she were to identify the local magistrate and his purpose in coming here."

"Did you keep it from her?"

"I have not told her anything about what people are calling the Meryton Murders. Georgiana does not read the news sheets—so unless somebody disobeys me and informs her, she shall not know until I judge her old enough not to be excessively distressed. As a result, I have had no call to tell her of Mr. Allwood and the many others I met." I breathe in her scent and study the gold flecks in her eyes. "I hope that I do not discomfort you when I say that I had mentioned *you* in my letters to my sister before ever I left the country."

She blinks and looks away, answering quietly: "It does not discomfort me. At all."

In the room around us, the gentle patter of talk and laughter and punch being poured into crystal glasses continues. It rises and swells and all about are smiling faces and affectionate glances. I even observe Mrs. Hurst squeeze her husband's arm as he gives his account of his club to Mr. Gardiner. Elizabeth and I are standing apart, by the window, and time is short. I grasp around for words, but Elizabeth finds them before me.

"I would ask you why Mr. Allwood calls here, Mr. Darcy, but I believe you may think my question interfering?"

"You may ask without risking my good opinion of you. That is quite intractable, Miss Bennet. It shall take more than an inquisitive turn of mind to move it."

She laughs gently, and it gives me confidence.

"So, since you have asked, I shall answer. I hope that this does not cause you discomfort either. If it does, I shall never mention it again, but I am afraid that I cannot deny it. You may have surmised it your-self. The truth is that I have been assisting Mr. Allwood with his investigations."

"That is something that my family and all of our neighbours would be grateful for, if only they were aware of it."

"I hope that a resolution may be found, and that they may all be safe. I have the highest regard for your family and neighbours. But I believe I have thought only of you. It is that, alone, which drives me."

"Well"—the dark orbs of her shining eyes look down and words die on her lips before she seems to find her courage. Once again, she looks me squarely in the face. "That is a great compliment...and a welcome one."

The meaning of her words hits me and the space between us appears to contract. A wave of joy rises through my being. *She welcomes me.*

"You have no idea how I have longed to hear you say so. I had almost given up hope."

"I cannot have that, Mr. Darcy."

She touches my sleeve so lightly that the connection was barely made. I incline my head to her as I speak.

"There is so little time. In a moment, we shall be called into dinner. Do I have your permission to speak to your father as soon as may be? I should like to ask him if I may court you. I know that may sound obtuse since I have already asked, unsuccessfully, for your hand in marriage. But I am anxious that you should be treated properly by me. If I court you before everyone who knows you, there can be no mistake that you are the first choice of my heart. May I ask?"

I feel that I have been speaking for a century. She replies briefly but no less directly.

"You may, Mr. Darcy."

I hardly know the evening that thereafter unfolds, such is the excitement of my mind. All present wear a smile, every voice raises a laugh. When dinner is announced, the party rambles into the dining room: the ladies' fine skirts brushing against one another, the low bubble of Hurst and Gardiner and myself talking in counterpoint to the melodious feminine tones. When no eyes are upon us, Elizabeth touches her hand gently to my arm and I begin to feel the heat of the future radiate through me. At dinner, she sits beside me and I observe the beauty of her countenance. The meal is unusually merry and ends with Louisa Hurst and Georgiana playing duets and Elizabeth singing. Happy voices give way to jokes and laughter. They are more vivid, more joyous than I have ever before heard.

Is it the state of my own mind that makes it appear so? I realise that until this moment, I have been hiding from happiness, eschewing the glories of life. In such reveries does the first evening of my new life pass. The minutes give way to hours and the hour grows late. Mrs. Gardiner's head inclines towards her husband and after some whispering, they begin to take their leave. The realisation of the hour appears to take Mrs. Hurst at the same time, and she begins tugging at her husband's sleeve and agitating to depart. In the tiled hallway, bonnets are donned, and cloaks are retrieved to a chorus of clicking heels and spoken pleasantries. When the door is opened, the cold air of the gas lit night seems to bite us. A lone watchman stands opposite, eyeing the house and all about. I observe him scrutinising us for but a moment, before moving into the shadows. I bid farewell to the Hursts who walk arm in arm along the yellow tinged road for their own home. Mr. and Mrs. Gardiner thank us and clip down the steps of Darcy House where their carriage waits. To Elizabeth, I bow, and she curtseys as she allows me to take her arm and escort her to the carriage. The night is perishing cold, and her uncle's horses send funnels of cloudy breath into the air. For all that, my hand is warm as she touches it. I do not believe we are observed as I lift her gloved hand to my lips and kiss it. Thereafter, I stand, alone, for Georgiana has retreated within doors, and watch their carriage move away, along the road, past the gated gardens, and out of sight.

Her absence leaves an emptiness, and I realise that I am standing out in the night for no reason, while the servants shiver. As I mount the steps and enter, James shuts the door behind me with a heavy clunk and some recollection, long buried seems to wrestle through my consciousness. A wisp of a memory steals past me, and I am back outside under a winter morning sun. Stevenson is there—and others —but I cannot now recall who. Horses' hooves kick up dust. Trunks are fetched and carried. To my right, a man looks away, his profile plain against the green and wrought iron background provided by the square.

"Are you content for me to lock up now, Mr. Darcy, sir?"

The footman's voice cracks through my consciousness like a bell intruding into a dream. The spell is broken, and I am back to the present. I struggle against the clouds of my own memories to find the image again, to piece it back together like a broken mosaic. But it is gone.

"Yes, of course. Please do."

CHAPTER 11

IN WHICH MR. DARCY IS ASTONISHED

he engagement is announced between Mr. Charles Bingley, eldest son of the late Mr. and Mrs. Edward Bingley of Scarborough, and Miss Jane Bennet, eldest daughter of Mr. and Mrs. Thomas Bennet, of Long-bourn, Hertfordshire.

My eyes absorb the black news sheet print, and I feel a sense of events chasing up on me. I had been informed in advance of the announcement, of course. Bingley had sent me a note, arrived the previous day, and Elizabeth had also shared the news with me. She had whispered her sister's unannounced engagement in a secret moment as Mrs. Gardiner discussed flowers with Georgiana. This had been only yesterday, on the Gardiner's final visit to Darcy House before escorting Elizabeth home to Longbourn. The weather having improved, I was given to understand that Mrs. Bennet had demanded her second daughter be returned. The party came to Darcy House to take their leave and only Elizabeth and I are aware that I am to follow hard on their heels in very little time. Presently, I sit in the breakfast room, eating an egg while my sister exclaims loudly on the forth-coming nuptials of our friends.

"Do you think we shall be invited, Fitzwilliam?"

"I should hope so. Bingley has already asked me to stand up with him, so I think it a safe assumption."

"How marvellous. I am all anticipation to meet Miss Bennet. Is she as lovely as Elizabeth?"

I am about to correct her informal address when I see a spark in her eyes and detect an unfamiliar jaunt in her smile. I have underestimated her. She knows.

"No." I let a moment of silence slice between us and can see that she is near to bursting with excitement. "But she is a very pleasant young lady and I am sure you shall like her very much. I think it likely, Georgiana, that I shall be travelling to Hertfordshire in the near future. I anticipate that it would be appropriate for me to go alone. But that having been achieved, would you like to stay at Netherfield for a time? I am sure that the Bingleys would be delighted and it is very close to Longbourn. I am likely to be staying there myself."

"I should love to, Brother. You know I would. Oh Fitzwilliam, why linger? Why do you not go now?"

"There is business I must address first."

"Whatever can it be? I wish you would tell me where you are going and what you are about! You have been so secretive of late. It would serve you right if I were to follow you!"

I placed the news sheet flat on the table.

"You shall do no such thing. I am travelling this morning to Shropshire. There is something I must do there. I cannot explain it to you, but it must be completed before I can go to Hertfordshire."

"I cannot understand how anything can be more important than you following Elizabeth."

"Nothing is. And I shall. But I owe it to her and her family to undertake this task first."

She smiles, hesitates, and continues to eat her toast, indicating that she is satisfied, at least in part.

An hour later, as I sit back in my carriage and rattle out of London, past fine houses and unkempt cottages and ragged men selling wares by the road, I wonder what I might find in the country beyond. Stevenson, with whom I travel, is enjoying some time with his book, as he well deserves, but my own mind has no time for leisure. Allwood, I have not yet seen, but we have exchanged express letters and formed a plan. The road from Hertfordshire to Shropshire being poor, Allwood is anxious that time should not be lost by him travelling to and from London. It is decided that I will travel to Shropshire alone and unaided, establish what can be learned, and then make for Meryton. In my pocket, I have the miniature and Allwood's last letter to me in which he makes some suggestions for extracting information. Reaching in and touching both, I am reminded of my purpose. It occurs to me that I had lived in the world for eight and twenty years, and I have never undertaken a task for the good of people beyond my family and dependents. Until now.

The journey passes slowly as green field upon green field and thicket wood after stone-built village whistle past. Larger towns swell on the horizon, church spires reach up to a clouded sky as the carriage pounds further up country. The first part of the journey is familiar to me, of course, well acquainted as I am with the road north. But the tracks part, the vistas change, new sights appear, and I am in a part of the country quite new to me.

An anonymous night passes in an inn where I sleep most fitfully to the chorus of men in the public rooms below. At some time after midnight, when the roar has still not abated, alone in the darkness, I think. Many scenes saunter through my thoughts: the dinner at Netherfield, the sight of Elizabeth and the dead man, the clatter of tea at the Philips', the face of George Wickham as he confesses the truth. Puzzle laid upon mystery planted on ignorance. Just as I believe the revellers below to have quieted, a great roar of drunken laughter comes crashing through the floorboards. I can stand it no longer. Sitting bolt upright in the narrow bed, I throw off my sheets, light a candle, and sit before a blank sheet of paper at the tiny desk in the corner. The flame flickers on it and on me, and my thoughts range around the possibilities like a wild cat. Not knowing quite why, I pick up my pen and begin to write a list of names. Who had been there, however fleetingly; who had been near, whatever their station. Even if it seems an impossibility of timing, the name is added on the list. My eyes rest on each name. When could he have committed the act? What possible reason may he have had? Faces, familiar and disjointed, draw pictures in my head, and every time I consider giving up, I see *her*, alone, staring at me. I will not give up. I cannot.

Later, the morning sun blinks unkindly through the narrow window of my room. The sound of the revelry below stairs has been replaced by the changing of horses and the loading of carriages. Men call for assistance, dogs bark, and the new day begins. I immediately rise and am dressed by the time Stevenson appears with a breakfast tray. His eyes twinkle as he observes me having attended to myself, but he knows me too well to comment.

"Good morning, sir."

"Good morning, Stevenson. I hope you slept tolerably?"

"Well, sir. It was a bit on the rowdy side, but I managed to get a few hours."

"Yes, I believe I did too. Still, it does not do to mope. Let us be away from here as soon as possible. I believe we are only twenty miles from Harking?"

"That we are, sir, although I do not know the quality of the road. The weather is set fair though, which must be an advantage."

I quickly consume some bread and tea, acknowledging my own hunger for the first time since our arrival in this odd place. Stevenson glances out of the window and sets about arranging my belongings. He hovers in a manner that suggests he wishes to speak.

"Yes?"

"Well, Mr. Darcy. Might I ask where we are going when we reach Harking, please, sir? I'd like to know what to tell James."

I place the remains of the bread on my plate and meet his gaze.

"That is a good question, Stevenson, and one you may well ask. But I do not know the answer yet. My design is to meet the residents of Highweston Manor. But since I have no idea of their name nor any thing about them, the matter calls for some consideration. I hardly think I can simply appear and demand an audience. No. I believe that we should approach the house in a circumspect manner. When we reach the place, I suggest that we obtain lodgings and then enquire about the manor. Having said that, we are not doing anything wrong. I have every intention of returning the miniature to whoever rightfully owns it."

His grey eyes look doubtful and he says, "I see, sir," as he packs what remains of my belongings.

It sounds like a poor plan, but it is all there is. With this in mind, we board the carriage and set off. Stevenson has been correct with respect to the weather and although the roads are by no means perfect, they are passable. It is only three hours later that the carriage rolls into the village of Harking, nestled among the gentle hills like a creature in wait. Not wishing to draw attention to myself, I sit back in the carriage, but my eyes are alert to every sight. It appears to be a sleepy place of ordinary enough dimensions, not as large as Meryton, not as small as Lambton. The road in is framed by farmland and low cottages but before long, larger houses appear around a triangle of green, replete with a stony Norman church. A gaggle of children run across the green shrieking and a man leading a horse stops to observe our carriage with undisguised interest. I ask James to make a turn of the place in order that we might find our bearings. Painstakingly, I plot each building, each turn in the road, committing them to memory, conscious that I may need to know it in the future. The cottages, side by side, the blacksmith, the well-appointed rectory sitting beside the church. My eyes fix on the façade of an imposing, red-bricked house. It is, I should say, a shade smaller than Longbourn and not quite as attractive. The skeleton of a wisteria creeps over the top of the oak front door and a bare, tended garden whispers of flowers in summer. It is plainly the most prominent house in the village and I chalk it down as the manor I seek. Oddly, there appears to be no sign of life: the windows shuttered, the door closed, not a soul in evidence. I ponder this as the carriage draws up outside the village inn.

We alight and take a set of rooms for the night in the small, low inn where, it appears, we are the only guests. The landlord is a heavy man with a hearty laugh, anxious to please, and plainly surprised by the arrival of an unknown gentleman in this out of the way place. I am considering the business of finding out information when I overhear Stevenson employ his own not inconsiderable initiative. He leans against the bar, in conversation with a young, rosy cheeked maid as though such an expedition is an everyday occurrence.

"Nice, comfortable sort of place you have here. My gentleman is just stopping, short term like. On the way into Wales, visiting relations but we been going since London and the horses need a break."

"London? Good heavens, mister. I'd love to see London."

"You might be disappointed if you did. Filthy place. This is much nicer. What's your name?"

"Ethel."

"Ethel. I'm Jim."

I blink at this and turn my gaze away from them, ears eagerly listening.

"Anyways, I like a nice village. Say, that red-bricked house by the corner of the green—is that the manor?"

"'Tis. Very fine, is it not?"

"It certainly is Ethel. I thought that when we comes past. What is the name of the folks who live there?"

Interested, I seat myself by a window in the public room while their discussion continues.

"Turnerville be their name. An old family too. Old, and they was grand, once upon a time. The best 'ouse in the village it is, and further afield. But folk round 'ere say it be cursed."

Ethel whispers the last remark, almost as though it would harm her if spoken too loudly. Stevenson replies, affecting nonchalance.

"Cursed? Why ever do they say that?"

In the corner of my vision, he crosses his arms on the dark surface of the bar and leans into her, confidingly.

"Because of all the terrible things what 'ave 'appened to the family. Awful, it is. You couldn't credit it, but it's all true. They wasn't a bad lot. Bit strange maybe. But they seemed to 'ave such bad luck, if you know what I mean?"

"What sort of thing?"

"Well, it all started years back when the old master died suddenly.

One day 'e was fine, next 'e's turned up 'is toes. Well, the mistress took it terrible. At first, everyone thought it was just grief, but before long, she run completely mad. People said they heard 'er raving and saw 'er gaddin' about the village in 'er nightclothes. Dreadful it was."

"Sounds it."

"But that wasn't all. For the poor lady died, leaving 'er three children. But people started saying that they was mad as well. That it run in the blood, like. The girl, who was a sickly creature, was married. But 'e was a funny one. One day 'e clean disappeared without a word. Next thing, 'er brother disappeared too, and then she follows 'im!"

"And nobody knows where these people have gone?"

"Not a soul. It's the talk of the village."

"That's a story alright, Ethel. Very odd. Anyone left in the manor now?"

"Only one. Young master Turnerville. But 'e lives there with 'ardly a stroke of 'elp. 'As a daily come in to cook and clean but 'e don't speak to 'er and nobody else goes into the 'ouse. Sad really, for 'e's a young man. And that 'ouse used to see balls and grand carriages visitin' and all sorts. 'Sall wrong, for it to be shut up like a mad 'ouse."

"I agree, Ethel. It sounds like a tragedy. Oh well. Maybe one day the young master will marry a nice girl and start living like a regular gentleman?"

Ethel laughs in agreement. And with that, Stevenson takes his leave from her and returns to me.

"Well done, Stevenson." I congratulate him quietly as he sits beside me.

"Thank you, sir. Shall I try showing her the miniature? She might recognise the lady."

"You could, but I think not for the moment. Ethel has told us something of the Turnervilles. But she was very eager to talk, was she not? I am inclined to err on the side of caution."

He glances in the direction of the young girl who is polishing tankards behind the bar and, I wager, watching our every move.

"I am here to establish information and possibly return an item to its owner. I do not wish to become a subject for gossip myself. We will come back to Ethel if we need to."

~

The church and rectory are a short walk across the green, which I undertake while Stevenson rejoins Ethel at the bar in the hope of local gossip. My coachman James walks heavily beside me and wrings his hands as I ask him to loiter behind when we reach the building. The church seems to me as good a place to start as any. But, of course, I have no idea whether I will find friend or foe there. I am a perfect stranger in this village, situated in a region where my family name and lineage mean nothing. Nevertheless, I press on hopefully, James a few steps behind me. Striding through the lychgate, I observe an elderly woman tending a grave, and as she looks up in surprise, I slow my step, chastened. The heavy, weathered door opens to my touch and within stands a stout, ordinary sort of font and a short, narrow nave with pews laid out on each side like regular branches. Stained glass casts colourful shapes into the space. It appears a typical country church. Observing nobody within, I begin to ramble around. The alter is small, and the pulpit empty. I make a progress around the transepts where memorial stones to local families and past rectors are mounted high. Names and dates are carved in stone, most but not all unknown to me, for there are a number of Turnervilles. This dusty corner could be any village in England. For was not the country full to bursting with tiny hamlets, squat churches sitting on village greens, and alehouses manned by bored young ladies?

I have no notion that I am not alone until a voice sounds from behind me.

"It is an attractive church, in its way, is it not, sir? Of course, it is far from remarkable. But it has many features to recommend it. And I must say, it is a pleasure to see it admired."

The clergyman, who is grey haired and leans on a stick, advances towards me from the direction of the vestry. I am about to interject with words of compliment when he continues.

"Of course, many people enter in, but so few really look. It is, perhaps, the serendipity of the stranger in any place, that he actually *looks* at things. Sometimes, it is the stranger who sees objects for what they are, while the locals carry on in the oblivion of familiarity. But, I digress—"

The cleric pauses and, with some physical effort, bows, before returning his eyes to mine in an expectant manner. I repay the civility and introduce myself.

"Mr. Darcy? Yes, I have heard of Darcys. Are you from the North? Yes, yes. I have some recollection, but at my age, my mind is rather unreliable. I am pleased to meet you, Mr. Darcy. My name is Fellowes, Reginald Fellowes."

At various times, I nod and try to speak. But I find it impossible to get a word in between his. He prattles on and I begin to look for ways to escape.

"I say, you are a tall man. May I ask you to remove a book from a high shelf in the vestry? I have been seeking a man such as yourself for weeks, for I cannot reach it."

"Of course, sir." I follow the hobbling reverend into the window-less room. His book is easily obtained for him and he continues to talk for some time, speaking of his obligations to his flock and the difficulty of finding people to assist him with reading now that his eyes are failing. "What I need, Mr. Darcy, is a young apprentice. A protégé, if you will."

"Does your church not have a curate, Mr. Fellowes?"

"They come, and they go. Presently, it is only me to serve the whole parish."

He laughs nervously and taps his stick rhythmically upon the stone floor.

"Have you been the vicar of this parish long, sir?"

"Good heavens, yes, Mr. Darcy. It is quite thirty years."

More than my lifetime. If this man cannot help me, then surely no man can.

"Mr. Fellowes"—he shuffles closer to me as I speak, interested

—"this may seem a somewhat odd enquiry, it may seem almost impertinent..."

"Never mind what it seems. I am old and I know that matters may be very different from that which they seem. Get on and ask it, sir."

With this prompt, I reach into my pocket and slip the smooth solid object from the handkerchief I have wrapped it in, before presenting it to him in my palm.

"Do you happen to know anything of this young gentlewoman?"

I take care in how I describe the lady, for of course, the truth is that I know nothing of her or her place in life. Mr. Fellowes leans forwards on his stick to examine it and a flicker of recognition comes across his face like a change in the weather. The features of his lined face still and for a moment, he simply looks. Thereafter, he draws a deep breath and peers at me, eye to eye. Silence crackles between us and I feel the weight of my ignorance to be a significant disadvantage.

"Do I detect in your expression, Mr. Fellowes, some recognition?"

"You do. Forgive me. I am slightly overcome. You see, sir, I did not envisage seeing her again. I had given up hope. She was never well, you know, but sickly. My conclusion had been that the poor girl had been so brutalised by misfortune that she was truly lost. She has been gone from here for some time. So long, that people are ceasing to speak of it. And that is always a bad sign, is it not?"

A gentle smile came to my lips, for I know just what he means.

"It is. I am myself, not a gossip nor do I believe you are, sir. This likeness does not belong to me. It has fallen into my hands, by a series of extraordinary events, the details of which, I am afraid that I am bound to keep to myself at this moment. But I am anxious to find the lady."

"That, I cannot assist you with."

With this, he turns and begins to move papers about on the vestry desk.

"You do not know where she is now, but do you know where she was? Where she has lived and where her people are?"

"Her people? Ha! That family, Mr. Darcy, has been cursed with a torrent of ill luck. They have suffered all manner of ill-deserved

152

assaults by life. And I shall not be the one to publish their misfortunes to strangers."

"And that does you credit, sir. I quite understand. Are you able to tell me where I may find some of her family or friends? Are they here abouts?"

"Not anymore, sir." He speaks impatiently, moving me towards the door and plainly calling the interview to an end.

"Mr. Darcy. I do not know your motives and I have no reason to think ill of you. But the child depicted in that bauble you have in your hand is one I have known from babyhood. And it pains me to say that I know not where she is now or whether she is safe and well. That is my failing. But I am afraid that loyalty forbids me from discussing her circumstances with you."

"I understand, sir."

I do understand. No person comprehends loyalty and silence better than I.

"Can you tell me her name?"

"Her name...to me, always Emma."

It is not her Christian name I seek. But somehow, the softness with which he speaks it and the strange misplaced intimacy of knowing it, confounds me. Having spoken, Mr. Fellowes limped out of the dusty church and into the green envelope of his village beyond. After a few moments of thought, I emerge to find him gone. John, faithfully stands outside. The lady who had been tending a grave is finishing her work and bobs a curtsey to me as she makes her way out of the churchyard. Wearily, I pace back in the direction of the inn, only to encounter Stevenson on my way. We greet one another, and he falls into step beside me. I dismiss James, who returns to the horses and address my dependable valet.

"Have you learned anything further?"

"No, sir. I know nothing of the manor house that you did not over-hear yourself. Apparently, the house has a master, but he shuts himself away. It is a rum do, if you ask me."

"It certainly is. The house looked to be completely shut up when we passed it. He obviously does not welcome visitors. But I am afraid that it cannot be helped. Let's go to it."

With that, we amble across the green, past the inn and towards the somewhat forbidding sight of the house. It stands before us, framed by leafless trees, almost shivering in the chill of the air. The front door and the windows alike are shut up and seem to proclaim a lack hospitality as loud as may be. For all that, the gate is slightly ajar, allowing Stevenson and I to slip through onto the gravel path. Smoke thinly billows from a chimney at the back of the house, like a secret breath. There is somebody here. They may not wish to be found, but they are within these walls. Wordlessly, Stevenson and I agree on silence as we advance. I knock upon the door. The volume of the heavy knocker is great indeed, and it is surely loud enough for anyone inside to hear. Wordlessly, we wait for it to open, anticipating its owner for some time before Stevenson speaks.

"Should you try again, sir? Maybe the person within is in the wrong part of the house?"

I cannot imagine that is true but do as he suggests nonetheless. Again, the sound of it booms about like thunder and we wait. Involuntarily, my feet begin to pace, and I find myself looking about for evidence of life. I look to Stevenson and know our thoughts are alike.

"They must have heard. It was loud enough."

"Shall I check around the back, sir?" His grey eyes flick towards the unknown prospect, just out of sight.

"Come," I say, setting off. "We shall go together."

Without losing further time, we pace around the perimeter of the house. It is larger than it appears from the front but is a sad and untended spectacle of a place. The frozen ground cracks beneath our feet and before long we round on a small door. I knock again, this time with my knuckle and when nobody comes, Stevenson steps back to observe the smoke swirling up above our heads. It is as he does so, that I hear a crack, the unmistakable sound of a branch breaking under the foot of a person, but it is not my valet. I spin around and in a thinly perceived moment, see the man before he gathers his wits, turns, and runs. On instinct, we follow him, pounding the icy earth and ducking under bare bracken, moving farther and farther from the house. We tear past splintered branches, arms thrashing, ragged breath sawing through the frosty air. I try to observe the man's features, lest I lose sight of him, but it is impossible. Of course, he has an advantage on us. He knows where he is and where the winding country track upon which we find ourselves leads. He appears young and reasonably fit and every now and then he ventures a glance over his shoulder, hoping no doubt to see us losing speed and falling behind. But Stevenson and I keep our pace. I have disadvantages enough, but speed is not one of them and I have no intention of giving up. It is in one such moment, as his anguished face, barely visible in the fog of his breath and ours, looks back, that he trips and falls with a thud. The man moves to stand but not before Stevenson launches himself through the air and upon him, holding him down like a fugitive. The two men curse as the captive seeks to escape and Stevenson endeavours to prevent him. Between them, they struggle and after a short time, the man ceases kicking and begins to show signs of submission. Taking advantage, Stevenson skillfully shifts and turns him over to face us. I blanch, and my mouth opens, wordless, incredulous. For I have seen this face before, but in such circumstances as I could not now credit. Memories, long disparate, join in my mind. This is the face I recalled in that fleeting moment after Elizabeth's carriage pulled away in the dark. I first saw it outside Darcy House, the morning I left London for Hertfordshire. And I last saw it, dead on the floor in a lake of blood at Netherfield Park. This, is the face of the man calling himself Tom Partridge.

CHAPTER 12

IN WHICH THE BENNETS ARE SURPRISED AT HOME

I act swiftly and cling to the hope that matters may take their course with the least pain to those involved. It may be a forlorn hope, but there it is. Before departing Shropshire, I write an express to Allwood setting out the information I have, however incredible, including my own suspicions. I form the view that the "Emma" of whom the Reverend Fellowes speaks so fondly is by no means dead. If she is where I think she is, then she is in grave danger. With this thought, I make all speed to Hertfordshire. Through valleys and over hills, past inns and villages—all the time drawing nearer to where my heart has been for some time. I exhale in frustration and gaze out of the carriage window, willing the journey to end. The roads are good to us, as is the weather, and Stevenson, who knows the import of this matter as well as any man, has engineered our stops to be quick and efficient. Still, the time that passes grates on me. I cannot arrive in Hertfordshire quickly enough.

It is a moment to be praised when, at length, Netherfield Park comes into view and my carriage halts outside the door. We are no sooner stationary than I spring from the conveyance, bound up the steps, two at a time, and hammer upon the door. It is quickly opened by a waiting footman. Wilkins, standing within the airy hall, appears shocked by my appearance.

"Mr. Darcy, sir?"

"Morning, Wilkins. Is Bingley at home or Miss Bingley? I urgently need to see them."

"I am afraid the whole party is taking tea at Longbourn, sir. As a courtesy to the family of Miss Bennet. They departed Netherfield not thirty minutes ago, sir. What a misfortune."

He looks about in a despairing manner, as though the answer lay on the floor or upon the walls.

"That is fine, Wilkins. I shall go there."

"Mr. Darcy, should you like to refresh yourself, sir?"

"I do not have time but thank you."

And with that my journey unexpectedly takes on another leg. Ignoring the surprise of James, I climb back into the carriage and we are away for Longbourn; Wilkins stands at the door and watches me go as a man dumbfounded. It takes but minutes to reach the house. As I approach, my vision of Elizabeth grows stronger and more vivid. If she or anyone close to her is in danger, then I will protect them. I bound from my carriage to the front door and a young woman shows me to the drawing room. There, I am met by a phalanx of surprised faces, pausing over cups of tea.

It is a surprise, for I little expect such a crowd. A fire quietly roars in the grate and throws its warm light upon all five Bennet sisters and their parents, together with Bingley, his sisters, and Hurst, and Mr. Philips, and his wife. The maid announces me and closes the door upon us all. Silence aches about the room before I recall myself and bowing low, address the lady of the house.

"Mrs. Bennet. Please excuse my intrusion. I have only just returned to the area and thought to pay my compliments to your family, and in particular to Miss Bennet, to whom I give my congratulations." I nod, smiling to the elder Bennet sister who glows and thanks me. My eyes draw, as they surely must, to her sister Elizabeth beside her. In the throng of the crowded room, we exchange the smallest smiles, like secret tokens.

Bingley, who stands beside his betrothed grins broadly, and laughs, although there is no joke.

"Good to see you, Darcy. I did not realise we were to have you back so soon"—he pauses and his eyes flick from me to those around the room and back again. "Well, in any case, it is marvellous to see you."

Perfunctory greeting emanates from Hurst and Mr. Philips and the three younger Bennet ladies whom I note have been relegated to a tiny, inadequate chaise in the corner of the room. Without speaking, Elizabeth stands and fetches me a cup of tea. As I take the cup and saucer from her, she lightly and almost imperceptibly caresses my hand. Her mother, who sits on a chaise before the fire, finds her voice.

"Well, Mr. Darcy. What a surprise this is. You are most welcome, of course. Any friend of Mr. Bingley's shall always be welcome at Longbourn."

She appears to spit the words out rather than say them and having done so, turns her face away from me, as though the very sight of me offends. Embarrassment visibly washes over Elizabeth before she speaks.

"Mr. Darcy, have you had a long journey?"

"I have, Miss Elizabeth. I have been on the road for two days together. But it does not matter. It is excellent to see you. And your family."

"Two days of travel! Good gracious," exclaims Mrs. Bennet. "I should not survive it, indeed, I should not. Even in the most comfortable of carriages, it should be the most awful trial."

"It was not an easy journey, madam. And I admit to having travelled faster than I would usually choose to do. I was anxious to return to Hertfordshire."

If Mrs. Bennet wonders at this comment, she asks nothing. Elizabeth meets my eye for the most fleeting of moments.

Thereafter, the conversation moves on. Miss Bingley and Mrs. Hurst are blinking their way through Mrs. Bennet's speech on the subject of wedding lace when I became aware of movement at the front of the house. I turn to observe a carriage turning into the circle and making its way towards the house. It sways and creaks as it comes to a stop in full view of the assembled company and is greeted within to assorted cries of astonishment.

"More visitors!" Miss Lydia's face lights up with excitement and she nudges her sister Miss Katherine, who scowls in return.

"Whoever can this be? I do not recognise the carriage. What do you think, Mama?"

"I have no notion," Mrs. Bennet replies, waddling towards the window to join her daughter. Frantically, she fans her face, exclaiming about her nerves and imploring her husband, who peers over his spectacles.

"Good heavens," says Mr. Bennet, as the room observes the carriage door opening and its passengers step out. "I do believe that it is Mr. Allwood and Mrs. Clairmont."

Behind me a babble grows loud and ranges around. The voices of Mrs. Bennet and her younger daughters crescendo and merge.

"My dear, Mr. Bennet, I cannot countenance another interview with that man! He puts me so on edge. I simply cannot abide it."

"What a strange lady she is. Always wearing that odd, little veil. I am sure it does not become her at all. Why, one can hardly see her face, but it cannot be that bad."

"Fancy calling today, and together, in this way."

"With her maid, as well, Mama!"

"So, we are to entertain the maid as well are we! The cheek. And when I have visited her, she has said nary a word. I had to do all the talking myself."

And on it continues. The braying ebbs and flows. I become aware of Elizabeth moving behind and then beside me. We link eyes for a moment before I turn back to the view of the garden and behold the new arrivals. Allwood appears characteristically grim. His frock coat is in a shocking condition and the set of his expression even sterner than usual. Behind him emerges the lady, heavily clad in mourning. She is diminutive and moves unhurriedly, as though adrift on water. Miss Lydia is quite correct though, beneath the veil, one cannot discern her features. I watch the two of them making their way towards the door and a sense of despair sinks in my belly. The sound of the knocker on the front door cracks through the house. Inside the drawing room, the atmosphere shifts. I observe Miss Bingley and her sister exchange glances filled with derision, but then they sit back, as though aware that a matter of some import is about to take place. The ladies teeter between anxiety and anticipation and all attempts to drink tea are abandoned. In the expressions of Bingley, Hurst, Mr. Philips, and Mr. Bennet, I observe an unfamiliar nervousness. For myself, my heart races. What is Allwood planning? And why does he do so here, in this house? There is no time for thought and contemplation. The drawing room door opens with a swish upon the carpeted floor, the bemused housekeeper announces the visitors, and they progress into the crowded room like a pair of skittles.

Mr. Bennet steps forward and welcomes them.

"Mr. Allwood, Mrs. Clairmont. Please do come in. We are, as you see, somewhat cosy today. But you are most welcome."

Mrs. Bennet, who stands to greet the newcomers, plainly takes umbrage at this remark.

"Cosy? Mr. Bennet. The drawing room is a capacious one and easily large enough to entertain several families at once. I—"

"To what do we owe the pleasure, sir?" asks the man of the house, his brow furrowing above his spectacles.

"I fear that it shall not be a pleasure, Mr. Bennet. I am sorry to say that I visit this upon your house most unwillingly. But two men are dead and there is nothing else to be done. I am here to make an arrest, sir."

I feel rather than see Elizabeth stiffen beside me and her skirt lightly brushes my boot. It is the strongest urge of my heart to reach out and touch her. While she and I are completely still, the remaining company move in a swarm of collective astonishment. Mrs. Bennet falls in a partial faint upon her chaise, and Miss Bennet and Miss Mary leap to attend her. Miss Katherine and Miss Lydia gasp and clutch one another's hands while Mr. Bennet suggests an interview in his study. I see Philips flinch in the corner of my eye and his wife begins to complain of the heat. I know why Allwood is here, I know the fire that drives him, but this is not how I should like to see things done. There are ladies here—and innocent parties. When a beast is cornered, one can never know quite how he will strike out. For these reasons, I intercede.

"Allwood. I must agree with our host. Might I suggest that the gentlemen retire to another room. I do not believe you have any business with the ladies here present?"

From behind me, the voice of Miss Lydia complains that she does not wish to miss "it" before being hushed by her eldest sister.

"I quite see why you suggest that, Darcy. But it is not quite accurate. If you will allow me, Mr. Bennet. I have fetched this lady with me for a reason. And I explicitly want an audience."

He turns and moves aside such that the placid Mrs. Clairmont comes into the view of the room. She says a breathy "good morning" as her gloved hands reach to her face and swept back the veil to reveal a young, finely featured face, at once new and familiar. During my long journey from Shropshire, I had many hours to think. In romantic and hopeful moments, I had come to suppose that the mysterious Mrs. Clairmont had no role in this affair. I had deluded myself that she was an innocent and unconnected widow leading a blameless life in the countryside. Now, it is plain to me that I was wrong. I look to the eyes, the slightly upturned nose, the set of the mouth; but I already know them. For this is the lady in the miniature, as plain as may be.

"This lady? What an expression, Mr. Allwood!" Mrs. Bennet stood as she gestures to her neighbour to sit.

"Thank you, Mrs. Bennet. I am much obliged to you. And I am deeply sorry to have deceived you and your family, and your many friends and neighbours. But I must tell you, that Clairmont is not my name. I am no more Mrs. Clairmont than you are."

Incomprehension dances across Mrs. Bennet's face and she fetches her hand nervously to her breast. The lace on her cap begins to flutter and she looks to her husband.

"Then who are you, please, madam?" he demands, no doubt fearing the answer.

"My name, is Mrs. Hurst."

The words rang out clear and simple and were greeted with silence as she turns and locks Hurst with a glare to pierce the heart. For a moment, the room hangs in suspense. Thereafter, the younger ladies let out gasps and whispers as Mrs. Bennet begins to prattle.

"How is that? How can that be? Why, it is impossible. It is nonsense, for this is Mrs. Hurst. I—"

All eyes fall on Louisa Hurst, stock still upon the chaise in her pink silk frock. Her left hand begins to shake, hardly at all, and then with great speed as her visage whitens. At length, she turns her eyes to her husband.

Mr. Bennet steps forward to stand beside Bingley.

"Mr. Allwood. I cannot claim to understand this. But I insist that this interview be conducted elsewhere."

Allwood turns to his host and addresses him, but I do not take my eyes from Hurst himself. I see a man I have known for some years. A man I believed I knew for a simple soul. His body appears to flinch. His eyes are wild, flitting from the standing lady in her black dress to Louisa looking up at him imploringly to the room of bystanders, wondering, speculating. His being tenses like a fox on the field and he mutters "forgive me" before bolting for the door. He makes the length of the drawing room in a flash, knocking over Mrs. Philips' tea and pushing past Mr. Bennet. Allwood darts after him in a haze of brown, but he is too slow. I run the short distance to the drawing room door. Hurst looks at me, disbelieving as I catch the villain and he jerks roughly in my grip.

"Stop struggling, man. There is no purpose in it. We know."

Hours have passed since the scene in the drawing room and I am alone in the Longbourn garden, turning matters over in my mind. I recall it now as one might an unsettling dream, where matters are both familiar and wildly out of keeping with reality. No sooner had I apprehended Hurst, then Stevenson arrived, together with the constable whom Allwood had apparently fetched with him but kept concealed so as not to alarm the house more than necessary. Hurst's large frame jolted slightly as he was held in shackles and led to the carriage to be borne away. Behind him was left a house in uproar. Mrs. Bennet's talking gave way to weeping and before long, shivering as though from cold, she was led above stairs by Elizabeth and her younger daughters. Mrs. Philips was taken ill with the hysterics and escorted to her carriage by her husband who spoke hardly at all and looked about the room furtively as he took his leave. Bingley's sisters sat beside one another, unmoving, beholding the room as though it were an unchartered land. Miss Bennet knelt at the feet of her betrothed's sister Louisa and clasped her hands. She seemed to know that it was not a moment for formal addresses, and nobody seemed to mind.

"You have had a shock. Shall I get you a drink? Should you like to lie down? We are at your disposal."

Still the lady moved not but sat rooted on the chaise as though she had been painted upon it—a picture of perfect composure. The only indication of emotion was in her eyes which flared and glistened as they beheld Emma Hurst standing in the middle of the room like a rock in a stream. That lady stared back, equally unmoving.

It was Louisa who broke the silence, although her voice cracked as she spoke.

"When?"

Emma Hurst fingered her skirts and tilted her head, giving every appearance of calm.

"Of course, you want to know some details, and you are entitled to that. We were married on third of April. 1808."

Miss Bingley gasped and clutched at her sister's hand. Bingley himself went to speak but no sound came from him. I recall wishing with all my heart that Elizabeth were present, for she would surely have known what to say. As it was, only the newcomer spoke:

"Hurst was known to my family for many years. His father had a small estate some miles from ours. He was an only child and his mother was dead, so they made for a lonely pair. But the estate was well husbanded and fertile. It still is. Ours is a quiet, out of the way sort of place where there is little society. There are few suitors and one must make do with what there is."

"And Hurst was your suitor?"

"I came of age. My father approached his father. There were afternoon visits and dances at country assemblies and the thing was done."

At this, the lady's fingers, which had been playing with the folds of her dress, threaded together in a white knot, jerkily.

"We had been married for a year when his father died. I thought he had no other family. But it transpired that I was wrong. For a year later, a distant aunt died, leaving him a great fortune. Far greater than he had ever expected, I believe. From then on, he was quite lost to me, although I could not know how lost. His mind was taken up by fashion and the fashionable. Money was spent lavishly, limitlessly, but not on me. Hurst told me his standing as a wealthy gentleman took him to London. He said that it was required of the fashionable and well-appointed to linger in Town rather than languish in the countryside. And so that was what he did. At first it was visits to tailors and meetings with lawyers. That is what I was told at any rate. Whatever took him to London, he stayed for longer and longer. When he came back, it was for ever diminishing snatches of time. And then, one day, he climbed into his carriage, and he did not return. I had long suspected that he had a mistress, but I little thought that he had taken another wife."

Her words had turned to a quiet sob and a tear broke from her eye before she turned to the fire and stared into its orange glow. "Forgive me," she whispered.

Fascination and horror bounced palpably between them and seemed to trap us all. I had sought to free us from it for I knew how the story ended. It would benefit Emma Hurst naught to tell it nor Louisa to hear it in that moment.

I coughed and approached the first Mrs. Hurst.

"Madam. We have not been introduced, but I am Mr. Darcy. I wonder if I might offer you my carriage to return to your home? I am conscious that Allwood brought you and he himself has now left. My carriage is outside, and my servant Stevenson shall accompany you."

After a short silence, Emma Hurst moved her eyes from the Bingley sisters and addressed Miss Bennet and myself.

"Thank you, sir. I have known many dangers. I have had the worst manner of deception practiced upon me. And I do not fear a brief carriage ride in the countryside. But thank you." She paused, drew a deep breath, and I believe I saw the shadow of a smile dance across her aspect as she beheld Louisa. "I shall be away. Good day."

With that perfunctory farewell, she curtseyed, turned, and quit the room.

Thereafter, Bingley and I had absented ourselves. The room, so crowded before, had emptied of people. Only Jane Bennet and the Bingley sisters remained in the new quiet. They huddled towards one another like true sisters. Louisa gripped Miss Bennet and Miss Bingley entered the embrace. Silently, Bingley and I agreed that it was an intrusion for us to remain and so withdrew. We had passed a time in the chilly garden, wandering among the winter trees and frost spangled sticks that later in the year promise roses.

Bingley was silent at first but after some pacing, expressed his incredulity. It was not a conversation, rather a monologue which I accompanied him on in order to ease his loneliness. *"Damn it, Darcy, how can this be? How can we have been so deceived? I knew the man. I have never been so shocked in the whole course of my life!"* He continued in this vein for some time, and I did not interrupt him. I knew too well the feeling of having more questions than answers and I did not wish to deny him the experience of simply being astounded. At length, and after a good deal of pacing about the Longbourn garden, Jane Bennet appeared, framed in the doorway, before advancing towards us. She had put on a cloak which suggested to me that she intended to walk out of doors. Her pretty features were tense with worry, and so I indicated that she and Bingley should walk without me. I had lingered here, uninvited, for long enough and it was high time I departed. Miss Bennet assured me that was not the case and invited me to stay for nuncheon, although she acknowledged that it may be a curious affair, with Mrs. Bennet taken unwell and the Bingley sisters incommoded by shock. We three smiled briefly and I was pleased to see her calm as she threaded her arm through Bingley's. There were women who would have shrunk from an association with such a family. Ladies, who would have looked upon the early stages of an engagement as by no means binding and who would have sought to remove themselves from a man whose sister had been mired in scandal before their eyes. Miss Bennet, it appeared, was made of sterner stuff, and I was glad of it. The years ahead were unlikely to be smooth for either Bingley or his sisters. The lovers smiled at one another in the cold and I prayed that their affection would be enough to sustain them. Elizabeth, who had escorted her mother from the drawing room, had not reappeared. Considering the drama that had played out and the sight of Mrs. Bennet as she was borne away, I had little hope of seeing her second daughter even if I lingered at Longbourn for the rest of the day.

~

Thus, lamenting and now quite chilled, I make for the stables to return to Netherfield. Full of purpose, I stride across the gravel until I hear a familiar voice from behind, and it stops me.

"Mr. Darcy?"

Elizabeth, who has plainly been running, comes to a stop some distance away. Her cheeks are flushed, and she wears only a shawl to protect her from the cold.

"I saw you from the window. You are not leaving?"

"I am, Miss Elizabeth. I think I must." I should move quickly away, match action to words. But I find myself quite rooted to the spot. "For now."

She smiles and beneath the shawl, I see her shoulders ease. The winter sun plays over her comely features and a light wind blows her skirts forward. I cannot bear to see her standing in the cold, so I lift my hat, suggest she return to the house before bowing and turning away. I hear the determined tread of her feet as she walks after me.

"I must say, Mr. Darcy. This is a very poor courting indeed. This is not at all what my novels have led me to expect."

I spin about to find her suddenly closer and smiling playfully.

"Well, it is a very poor courting of a lady when a gentleman appears unexpectedly at the home of her parents when they are entertaining others. It is a disappointing manner of hero who ruins a family's peace by causing one of their neighbours to be arrested for murder in the middle of a morning visit. And what heroine wishes her suitor to bring such dramas to her door as to cause her mother and aunt to be taken ill? It is poor courting indeed. I am quite ashamed of myself as a romantic hero. In case I have not been clear, I believe I have given your family trouble enough for one day."

A smile twitches on her lips and her head tilts up in challenge.

"Is this your manner of suggesting that you would have gone about it in a different way?"

I could not but laugh at this.

"Yes, I suppose it is. I cannot speak for Mr. Allwood's methods."

"But you knew that Mr. Hurst was the murderer?"

"Yes, I did. I came here as soon as I knew he was here."

"You did have a somewhat wild look in your eye when you were announced."

"I am sorry about that, Elizabeth. It is not in my nature to be melodramatic. But once I knew he was here with you all, I could not countenance staying away. I had no idea that Allwood planned to appear."

"But you had been in contact with him, had you not? That is what you have been doing these last days. You have been assisting the investigation. And when Mr. Allwood came here, he was acting on information discovered by you?"

In the days spent away from her, I had almost forgotten the velvety, softness of her voice. I remember it now and it envelopes me. Silently, I languish in it.

"If you do not answer me, Mr. Darcy, then I shall take silence to mean consent."

"I thought it your design to have me speak more, not less? Since I am of a mind to consent to everything you suggest, you are defeating your own plan."

"I do believe you could speak more, Mr. Darcy. But not all the time."

She blinks and smiles as she speaks but her words send a spark of confidence through me. The history of our dealings with one another seems to career about in the space between us. The time for dissembling is well past. Swiftly, I step towards her and time stills as our lips meet. I am shot through by arrows of tenderness and anticipation and the warmth of her radiates through me. My hands fix on her arms, slip to narrow shoulders and thereafter cup the smooth planes of her face, like a rare jewel, found. Beneath my touch, she yields, and soft hands embrace me back. It is not a chaste kiss but searching and intensifying. The power of it roars in my ears and echoes through my body. A promise of lust eddies between us and I know that I must stop it. Planting my hand on her waist, I break away and kiss her forehead.

"Elizabeth, I am sorry. I am quite ashamed of myself."

"Ashamed?"

"Not of the act. But of the place."

She looks about her, as though unaware she stands in her parent's wintry garden.

"It could be warmer, I suppose. And perhaps, more private." A laugh plays about her mouth, but I cannot allow her to make a joke of it. This woman has seen me at my very worst and she is entitled to an account of it.

"I have a poor record with you, but I intend to correct it. When I first loved you, I was arrogant. I approached you as though I were entitled to you. Appearing here on the morning after your cousin had died and suggesting that your parents could not look after you adequately—it was shameful. Then, I learned to be more respectful, but I was still less than the man you deserved, because I had not proved myself. I was brought up with good values, Elizabeth, but I had never had to put them to work. They were like a book on the shelf that had never been read. After that, when you were in London and since, I have tried to use my skills and my advantages to bring about some good."

"I know."

"In some ways, I wish you did not. You deserve a respectable life, Elizabeth. Free from the stain of this business. As it is, you have happened upon a dead man and been questioned at length before everyone who knows you. Under my own roof, you have dined with a murderer, indeed, the murderer of your own cousin. If I could release you from this history, I would."

"You found out about Mr. Hurst. It was not Mr. Allwood who discovered his true character. But nobody knows your role."

"There is some truth in that. But it is no criticism of Allwood. He could not travel fast enough. We had information that somebody connected to this matter was residing in a place called Harking in Shropshire."

"Where did you find that information? In London, when you were away from Darcy House so much?"

"Yes. I was hunting for Wickham. I never believed him capable of murder. But I knew he knew something and eventually, I found him. His information led me to Shropshire. So, I went there. I had never imagined doing such a thing and I was ill equipped for it, if the truth be told."

"You must have overcome that. For you appear to have unmasked a murderer. How ever did you discover him?"

"I went to Shropshire with little on my side. Wickham had given me a miniature of a nameless young woman and an address. It was soon established that her name was Emma Hurst, née Turnerville, a native of the village and a gentleman's daughter. People spoke of her parents having died and her husband having abandoned her. She was said to have been left with only her twin brothers for comfort and company. After a time one of the twins—an Edwin Turnerville also disappeared from the village and some weeks thereafter, so did Mrs. Emma Hurst. The local people speak of this family as though they were cursed, such is the extent of their misfortune."

"But Mrs. Emma Hurst was here?"

"Yes. She was here. And before her, her brother Edwin. It appears from what his surviving twin told me that he travelled first to London and thence to Hertfordshire, seeking out his faithless brother-in-law. I know not how he found Hurst, but he did. He wrote to his siblings, you see. As soon as I saw the body of the first victim, I had a sense that

I had seen his face before. It was only much later that I recalled seeing him in Grosvenor Square the morning we departed for Netherfield. It had been some weeks before and seemed so unconnected with the murders, but there it was. It would appear that he followed us to Meryton and obtained employment at Netherfield as a means of being close to Hurst."

"And what was his intention?"

"We cannot know. His twin brother swears that all he wanted was justice. He may or may not be romantic in that interpretation. Turnerville may have intended to blackmail him. Hurst has a private fortune. Or he may simply have wished to disgrace him. Either is possible. It turns out that much more than I credited is possible. I never thought it possible that I would be easily deceived by a well-cut frock coat and a louche manner, but I was. I never asked any questions about Hurst even though, when one thought about it, very little was known of him. He was wealthy to be sure but appeared to have no family. I was told that his family were either passed or living far away and I simply accepted it. Twelve months ago, he and Louisa were married in London by special license, so the banns were never called. And even if they had been, the villain was so far away from his wife and family that they would never have known to object in any case."

She blinks and sighs, looking about at the ground. It is a great deal to comprehend.

"You see, I had always discounted the possibility that the murderer could have been one of the party at dinner. You may have thought me prideful—"

"Not now. My view of you is quite changed, as you know."

"Yes, I do. But before it was not so charitable, quite justifiably. But it was not a case of conceit. I took that view because at the inquest, Mr. Smee said he had seen the dead man alive and well at eight o'clock. But of course, I had not reckoned on the fact that he had a twin."

"His twin was at Netherfield?"

"Yes, for a time he was. They must have worked very carefully to conceal that, and I do not believe that Hurst was aware of it. But he was there, and I believe that it was he whom Smee observed. After his brother's murder, he ran away. Dressed as a vagrant, I shouldn't wonder. I believe that Hurst killed Turnerville just before dinner. You recall your brief time in the library?"

Her large eyes flicker. "Yes, I do."

I take her ungloved hand in mine and squeeze it as she looks out over the garden. For a time, she leans into me in silence.

"But how can Mr. Collins be involved in this matter?"

"By a series of misfortunes and cruel happenstance. It appears that by way of George Wickham, the miniature I spoke of fell into the hands of your cousin. It had been brought to the village by Edwin Turnerville and once he was dead, it was the only link between these murders and Emma Hurst in Shropshire. I believe that Hurst observed Mr. Collins showing the miniature to people at your aunt's party. He must have poisoned his drink. It is the only explanation."

"Could he be so depraved that he carried poison upon his person? I think he must be mad, quite mad."

"I believe you are right. By this point, he is likely to have been crazed with fear that his history and his crime would be discovered. This is another matter about which we may never know the truth."

"You cannot blame yourself for that. You have discovered so much. You, yourself, acting alone."

"Yes, I did. I never imagined myself doing such a thing. But I also never imagined that matters could be as they were—that a man I believed I knew had deceived all who were connected with him. I searched for the truth, every hour, every moment, wishing myself with you. But I could not come here having gained nothing. When the villain was unknown and at large, I could not give up."

Elizabeth exhales a misty breath in the winter air and regards me frankly.

"I hope you know that I would never have brought this upon your family in the way that Allwood did. Bringing the lady here and cornering Hurst in your drawing room."

I pause, thinking, but not saying that it was an enormous risk. Allwood had no idea how Hurst would react. "It was excessively dramatic. It was callous. Any person who has met your mother would know that she would be most distressed by it."

She half-smiles at this and edges closer still. Her clothing brushes against mine and our breath mingles in the air before us. I could be unravelled by it.

"That is true. But Mr. Allwood does not concern himself too much with the feelings of others. It is the reason that he is held at a distance by so many. But it is also an advantage to him as a magistrate—it allows him to hold others at a distance, does it not?" She reaches out and touches her gloveless hand to my arm. A melting feeling stirs within me, a sense of an ending forms in my mind like a grand painting. For a moment, I simply behold her hand in mine, feel her body pressing subtly against me. She shifts and threads her arm through mine.

"Yes, you are right. But I am not here as the local sheriff, Elizabeth. You know my feelings for you, and my intentions."

"And you know mine. They have not changed. They have only grown."

She tightens her grip on my arm and a spark lights in her eyes as she smiles. In silence, at the side of the house, alone, we stand. Her eyes not leaving mine, she slides her hand down my arm slowly. As she reaches my wrist, I take her hand in mine as she continues. "And how could they not? Think of what you have done for us. You have pursued the truth relentlessly, where no one else would. For the protection of others, you have consorted with a man who has wronged you. You have secured the arrest of a dangerous criminal. But it is more than that. You have assisted a community of people with whom you have no connection, no loyalty. We are not your people, and yet you have helped us. And when it became clear that the offender was from among your own set—you did not flinch from your purpose. And so, Mr. Darcy, how could I not know you for the very best of men?"

"I do have a connection with your people. What greater connection could I have than you? I only wish I had treated you differently at the beginning of our acquaintance."

"Well, if that is your only regret, sir, then put it from your mind."

She takes my other hand and no man could mistake the welcome in her eyes or the conspiracy in her expression.

"You are not offended then?"

"I am not offended, Mr. Darcy."

She links her arm with mine once more and begins to walk. I have no choice but to walk with her and I want nothing more. Expertly she steers me away from the stables into a wooded wilderness to the north of the house. The ground beneath our feet crunches as we move into the darkened glade.

"It is time, I believe, to turn a new page. I feel sure that in the weeks and months to come, we shall learn more of this affair. But it shall not define us. We shall move on. We shall be the happiest of couples. I know it to be so."

The wind blows, sending her chestnut hair coursing about her face and neck and she laughs, pushing it back.

"We cannot remain out here, Elizabeth."

"Can we not?"

"No. You are not dressed to be out of doors. And I would never wish for anyone to think you compromised by me. You are worthier than that. I suggest that you return to the house."

I kiss the top of her head, and she looks up expectantly. "And you?"

"I shall follow after. I had thought it better to wait, considering what has passed here today. But now, I think differently. Your father is at home. If you agree, I should like to speak with him now?"

She nods. "You know I agree. I told you in London."

"But London was London, and now we are here. You agreed to me requesting permission to court you. Now that I have kissed you, Elizabeth, I do not know that I can bear to wait. If I may, I intend to ask him for your hand."

Glancing about her, almost imperceptibly, she stands on the tips of her toes and reaches for my face as she whispers, "You may."

CHAPTER 13

IN WHICH THE MISTRESS OF DARCY HOUSE AWAKENS

I re-fold the letter and rest my eyes briefly on the square outside the window. London awakens later than the country, but the activity of the day is well underway now. Carriages click about, servants rush from here to there, the households they serve judder to life. Newsboys walk hopefully, calling out stories, steps are cleaned and glisten in the early spring sun. Men and women chance guilty glances at that house not far from this one. They shall go unrewarded. The property has been shut up for weeks and shows no sign of the recent tragic drama. Passers-by may look, but they shall see nothing. I exhale, I believe from relief. After all that has happened, I believe our work here is done, and I shall be glad to get away.

A soft sound comes from across the room and in the bed my wife stirs. Framed by the great pillars of mahogany and the richly coloured canopy, her body looks small. The shape of her shifts about beneath the counterpane and her blanket of dark curls, tangled from the night's lovemaking, moves on the pillow. Suddenly, a creamy arm appears.

"Fitzwilliam?"

She blinks as her eyes adjust to the light and pushes herself up on one elbow. The covers fall away and pool around her form, which is unclothed beneath them.

"You are dressed. Is it late?"

"No, my love. At least not by your recent standards. It is nine o'clock."

"Nine o'clock!" Elizabeth shrieks playfully. "If I had stayed abed until nine at Longbourn my parents would have summoned the physician." She smiles and pushes the pillows up against the headboard before leaning against them. The morning light seems to bounce off her. "Laying in bed until this hour, we might almost be mistaken for members of fashionable society."

"You may speak for yourself, Elizabeth. I have been awake these two hours."

"Hmm. You have a habit of secretly working, I believe. But I thought that all our plans were arranged, and all preparations made. What more is there to do?"

She raises her eyebrows, knowing full well that she is right. I grip the letter in my hand tighter, but I cannot keep its contents from her for long.

"Nothing, to be truthful. The servants have seen to our packing. Georgiana is to stay on in Town, so there is no need to shut up the house. All is ready for our departure. I observed young John polishing the carriage yesterday, no doubt in anticipation of the journey."

"He is getting on well, is he not? It was a wonderful idea of yours to take him on."

"He is a good boy. I trust that he will prosper better at Darcy House than he would at Mrs. Younge's. He was only too pleased to leave that establishment. When I asked him, he looked fit to burst."

She laughed and stretched out her arms.

"Good. As well he might. That is a happy ending nobody could have anticipated, least of all John. I wonder if we shall ever have dealings with Mrs. Younge or Wickham again? I hope not, for your sake. For I believe that you have suffered them enough."

I had pondered the same question myself. It is a relief to discuss it.

I never thought to find a wife with whom I could share confidences and debate ideas with such ease, but I have that privilege now.

"I cannot predict the future, but I doubt that we shall hear of Wickham. Searches were made for him, but they turned up nothing and the army consider him vanished. For my own peace of mind, I had Stevenson make some enquiries at the docks. We can never be sure, but I believe it likely he is gone abroad. I doubt that he shall return."

"So do I. But let us think of him no more. For Wickham belongs to the past. Today looks to be a bright one."

She nods to the early spring light streaming through the window. A whimsical, joyful look dances about her and she leans back more, smiling broadly. The room is a calming haze of green and blue and a view of Pemberley hangs over the fire place. Since removing to London immediately after our wedding in Hertfordshire, we have slept every night in this room, the mistresses' chamber. Unbidden, my mind flies to the darkness of the night, to her form beneath the covers, to the feeling of her hands upon my bare shoulders, her breath against my face. If ever she was nervous or apprehensive about that portion of married life, she did not show it. She is just as bold in darkness as in light. Presently, she drinks some water from a glass by the bed, before pushing back the covers and perching, quite naked, on the edge. My breath draws in sharply to watch her reach for a dressing gown draped on a nearby chair and stand to put it on. Unaware of this reaction, she begins padding around the room, singing quietly before pausing before the painting over the fire.

"It seems so strange that I have been Mrs. Darcy these two months and have not yet been to Pemberley. I do not regret it, of course. We had to stay to assist the Bingleys and Mr. Allwood. I understand why. But it is singular, and I look forward to remedying it."

"You are not sorry to leave London?"

"Not excessively so. I am so thankful that we were in the South for Jane and the Bingleys when—it—happened. I should have been wretched if I had been far from her and I believe that we did help."

"Yes, you are quite right. Although Jane has behaved creditably.

There are few young women who could have managed so deftly the catastrophe that she has managed within weeks of marriage. Anyone of sense can see that."

"Yes, they can. But thank you for saying so." She smiles gently and then more brightly, and I know that she is in the throes of changing the subject. "London has been wonderful, of course. I never thought to walk in Hyde Park each afternoon or attend the theatre so often. Nor to receive morning calls from titled ladies."

Elizabeth tilts her head and smiles laughingly.

"Yes. I am sorry about Aunt Catherine. I am afraid that she is rather conscious of her position in life." I have already apologised to my wife, in more ways than one, for the rather less than enjoyable call paid by Lady Catherine de Bourgh during our first days in London. The truth is that our marriage happened so quickly that my aunt did not have time to make the trouble she may otherwise have made. And once it was done, it was done. Her only recourse was thinly veiled rudeness. "Let it console you that we are not spending Easter with her. I usually do, together with my cousin, Fitzwilliam. But I could not subject you to that only months into marriage and after everything that has happened."

"I know." Her bare feet peek beneath the gown and pad across the carpet towards me. I put the letter aside, anticipating her. She plants herself on my lap before taking my head in her hands and kissing me in a most deliberate manner. "I look forward to visits to Rosings Park. In the future."

We laugh at this notion. Privately, I think Easter next year may be the moment to take Elizabeth to Rosings. It should not be before, I am certain. My wife makes herself comfortable in my lap and for a time, we simply kiss. After a period, she chances a glance out of the window and stops.

"I see people are still pausing outside the house, as though there were something to see. How long shall it go on do you think?"

"Not long, I trust. Let us hope that the public memory is short."

"Poor Louisa. I understand from Jane that after everything, she has taken this latest shock most grievously. They had hoped that when

Mrs. Emma Hurst returned to Shropshire, Louisa would improve, but sadly she has made little progress towards recovery. Caroline hopes to persuade her to undertake a tour on the Continent. Apparently, an aunt and uncle from the North shall accompany them. But Jane does not believe that Louisa shall be able to face such a thing for some months."

"It is a shame. It is probably in her interests to change her surroundings."

"I know you are right, but it does not sound such a fine prospect. Shall she have to run all her life from scandal?"

Her intelligent eyes pause on the activity in the square as she speaks and we both know it is a good question.

"I hope not, Elizabeth. Everyone knows that she was not at all culpable. She knew nothing of Hurst's history. I told Lavinia Protheroe that Louisa knew nothing at all and was an innocent victim in the hope that the whole of London would soon hear the same. I believe my godmother has done her work. She has held soirees specifically for the purpose of propagating that piece of information. Let us hope that in time, people will forget, and Louisa may move in society again."

"Yes. The odd thing is that you have explained everything to me and still, I do not understand one thing. I can comprehend how he felt compelled to murder in order to protect his secret. It is quite depraved, but it is clear enough. But why did he marry Louisa, knowing that he had another wife? What madness led him to marry two wives?"

I tighten my grip around her and pull her closer. Elizabeth has made it plain that she does not wish to be kept in the dark about events.

"He did not say before—well, he did not give any explanation when he was questioned. For the most part, he refused to speak altogether. I believe that it was simple though. I believe that he loved Louisa. Did you never notice that they appeared unusually affectionate with one another?"

"I did. Their marriage seemed a happy one. But I did not think anything of it."

"When he came to London and began moving in fashionable society, he said nothing of his life in Shropshire, so nobody who met him in those days knew that he was married. Louisa was one of those people, deceived from the first. The most likely explanation was that he met and fell in love with her. Louisa Bingley was not the sort of woman whom a man may take as his mistress, even if he were that way inclined. To have gone about it in a lawful manner, he would have had to have admitted that he was already married and obtained a divorce. That is not an impossible feat, but it is expensive, lengthy, and uncertain. I rather suspect that he thought of Emma, sickly and living in the wilds of the countryside, far away from any of his new acquaintances, and he decided to take the chance. He was, in the final analysis, a coward of a man."

She nods by way of assent and pulls back, seeming to regard me. Her gaze is as appraising as it is loving.

"He was. Mr. Darcy, are you going to tell me what is playing upon your mind, or must I drag it from you?"

"Your abilities are uncanny, Elizabeth."

"They are not. It is you who cannot hide your anxieties easily. Please tell me what it is."

"I have had a letter from Allwood. You recall that your uncle Philips aroused some suspicions during the investigation?"

"Yes. You informed me of that."

"Well, the suggestion that he was in any way involved in the murders has been long since dismissed. However, you know how thorough Allwood is. He is like a dog on a scent. In any case, I am afraid that the misdeeds of Mr. Philips have now been established."

"And they are?"

"It appears that he and another solicitor have, for some time, been involved in a swindle."

Her face remains impassive, but I feel the tension in her body. It is another misfortune that her family little deserves.

"The arrangement appears to consist in the two men of law

targeting wealthy gentlemen and persuading them to invest in interests abroad. A diamond mine has been mentioned, as has land in the Americas. It would appear in all cases, they did not really exist. Philips and his partner retained the funds and then, after some prevarication, informed the investor that the venture had failed or suffered a dreadful loss. This charade was carried on through a partnership with an office in Town. It was presented to investors as a third party—and they were led to believe that Mr. Philips and his friend were merely intermediaries. And yet, there was no other party involved."

"Good heavens. Do you think that when Mr Philips came to Netherfield, he had Mr. Bingley within his sights?"

"I think that very likely. Allwood tells me that they particularly concentrated their efforts on young gentlemen, believing them to be naive. And they were no doubt diverted by the prospect of Bingley's wealth, which is considerable, and his aim to establish himself in the world."

"How appalling for my aunt and Mama. And how must Jane feel? I must write to her directly."

"Of course, he made no progress with Bingley at all. That may be, in part, due to the chaos created by the killings. Bingley was simply concerned with other matters. And when he was not dealing with those events, he was courting your sister. So, I do not believe that Philips came close to extracting funds from him."

"That is one thing to be grateful for. But how many others were cheated?"

"Allwood does not say. But I believe both men have been arrested and await justice. We shall have to see. I believe that we shall have to show friendship to your aunt, Elizabeth. She shall find herself at the centre of some scandal."

"Yes. More scandal. I am sorry, Fitzwilliam, for bringing such a history to your door. I little know what to say."

"Then, do not say anything. Unless I am mistaken, you were never fond of your uncle in any case?"

"No. How like you to have discerned that."

She leans in towards me and lays her head against my chest, like a cat bedding down before the fire. "I shall write to my aunt."

"Quite right. We shall afford her all the assistance we can. Whatever you think best."

My only answer is a soft kiss on the collar bone. She eases into quiet contemplation and although I have not lived with Elizabeth for long, I know well enough when she is thinking deeply.

"What an odd and unsatisfactory beginning to a marriage this has been?"

"I will give you odd. But I shall not admit unsatisfactory, Elizabeth."

"I do not mean to suggest that I am in any way unhappy. You know that is not the case. Rather, it is out of keeping with the idea of romance, is it not? One does not expect to meet one's spouse in such circumstances. There have been two murders and a bigamy. Now, we are told that there has been an elaborate fraud. We have both learned that those close to us may be quite different from what they seem. Dangerously different."

"Hmm."

"I cannot believe that you ever imagined meeting your future wife over a dead body?"

"I did not. But to be fair, we did not meet in that way. I was already quite beguiled at that point, as you know. In any event, what are you seeking to say?"

"Only that I wonder how matters may have proceeded had it not been for the drama that unfolded. Would our marriage have happened at all?"

"Of course. I stayed for so long at Netherfield for you, Elizabeth. And even if you had not been sent to London after the death of your cousin. I feel certain that I should have sought you out somehow."

"Maybe that is true." She kisses my collar again and a dart of heat shoots through me. "I cannot help feeling that absent the killing and tragedy, there may have been more dancing involved in the whole enterprise. Perhaps, had Mr. Bingley held a ball at Netherfield, I may have fallen in love with you there?"

"I wish I could say that would have been likely. But I am not at my

best in a ballroom. If you feel, my love, that you have had little dancing, then we shall have to hold a ball at Pemberley. What say you?"

"That is a wonderful idea."

"But for the moment, Mrs. Darcy, this is your final day in Town.
What would you have us do?"

"Well, I believe I have done my duty by the world at large. I spent
yesterday with my aunt Gardiner and gave our gifts to the children.
Mrs. Protheroe called the day before, and she is now gone to the
country, so I know she shall not be back."

"She will visit you at Pemberley. That I can guarantee. She thinks
nothing of travel and—"

"She wishes to check up on me?"

"Quite the reverse. She has already established in her mind that
you are suitable and a woman to be approved of. She shall assume,
correctly, that I intend to keep you to myself in the country and visit
the fog of Town as little as I may. So, she will visit you at Pemberley
on that alone."

"Well, I look forward to it. But she shall not come here today."
With this, she kisses the edge of my mouth, the silk of her eyelashes
curling against her cheek. "We have your cousin Fitzwilliam joining
us for supper with Georgiana. But other than that, I believe that the
day is our own." She kisses me again and I move against her in
response. My hands explore higher and the room spins and shrinks.
Still, Elizabeth is able to talk. "A last walk in Hyde Park, I should love.
But that is not in the way of an immediate need. The afternoon seems
to me to be an ideal time for such a venture."

"And the morning?" I croak.

"Let us remain here."

POSTSCRIPT

AN EXCERPT FROM A PAPER ON THE EARLY EVOLUTION OF THE METROPOLITAN POLICE BY PROF. BRIONY ZAIR DELIVERED AT THE LONDON SCHOOL OF ECONOMICS, 9 OCTOBER 2016.

*T*he subject of this talk is nothing more than a footnote in the history and development of organised policing in England. His is a name that many scholars are unaware of and there is no known image of him in existence. This is a narrative with many holes, but we, as historians know only too well, that they are often the best kind when it comes to elucidating the whys and wherefores of the past. It is the half-hidden men and women of history, the forgotten names and stories which, if found, may cast the brightest light on our world.

With that introduction, therefore, I present to you, Mr. Reginald Allwood, magistrate (b.1768-d.1840). First, the facts as far as we know them. Born in the early years of the reign of George III in a small village in Hertfordshire, Allwood came from a landowning, but by no means wealthy, family with powerful local ties. He was the eldest of his parents' five children and both his father and his grandfather before him had acted as local magistrates. He married in 1790, one

Emily Fisher, whose place of birth is listed on their marriage certificate as Ireland. Nothing is known of how Allwood came to marry a woman who was not English. However, what is known, is that when the eighteen-year-old Emily married, she was not long for the world. The records of St. George's Church, Meryton record the death, sixteen months later, of one Emily Allwood and an infant male, whose name has unfortunately been indelibly obscured in the original manuscript. It must be assumed that Allwood's young Irish wife died in childbirth, taking his son with her. He never married again, and nothing is known of the circumstances or consequences of what must have been a calamitous event. Such is the historian's lot, picking across the damaged landscape of human interactions, separating out the mundane and the heart-rending. Sometimes finding answers, sometimes not.

Some twelve months after the death of Emily, Allwood also lost his father and inherited the family estate of Rapcombe House, near Holwell in Hertfordshire. There he lived, as far as we are aware, for the remainder of his life. He became a magistrate in 1795.

There were, as you all know, many such gentlemen magistrates in England at this date. This is an expert audience, so I shall not set out a lengthy background history. You are all aware that in 1795 there was no organised police force in England as we have come to understand it and the landscape of law enforcement was one that we would hardly recognise. What, if anything distinguishes Mr. Allwood? What claim does he have, over two centuries later, to being considered?

There are, I would suggest four significant points of reference.

Firstly, in 1801, Allwood was praised in the Times for having apprehended and prosecuted one Samuel Jacks for the murder of a local goldsmith. This would be a standard story of a predictably solved crime, with an obvious motive, were it not for a number of factors. It appears, from the scant records in existence, that Jacks was a previously respectable member of the community and had known his victim well. This was not an instance of the "travelling vagrant" so common in the annals of early 19th century British criminal history. Early reports of Jack's arrest suggest that there was significant protest from another Justice of the Peace and a local Lord. So, what does it mean? Why do we care? I suggest to you, tentatively, that Allwood looks and smells different to other magistrates of the period. He does not just round up the usual suspects and have done with it. He is a new creature.

Secondly, and most famously (if the world "famously" may be permitted in discussion of a subject entirely unknown outside a small and specialist selection of scholars), in 1811, he was responsible for solving one of the most remarkable crimes of the period. The case concerned the murders of two, apparently unconnected men, in quick succession in the small Hertfordshire town of Meryton. On 14 November, a servant, later identified as Edwin Turnerville, was stabbed in the home of his master. Two weeks later, one Mr. William Collins, a young clergyman visiting relations in the area was fatally poisoned. A brief history of the case may be cobbled together by surviving newspaper reports and a brief document, written by an unknown (but not believed to be Allwood) which later came to light amongst the archives at Bow Street. It appears that Allwood conducted extensive investigations in which he took the unusual step of interviewing every living person—including all servants, no matter how lowly and all ladies, no matter how fine.

A number of suspects appear to have been within his view, ranging from senior servants in the home of the first victim, a local solicitor and a serving solider stationed in the area. The identity of the perpetrator, when Allwood revealed it, was a source of significant scandal. Mr. Christopher Hurst was the wealthy brother-in-law of the man in whose home the first murder had taken place. He was rich and socially connected, married to a woman who was likewise.

Quite how Allwood tracked down the information necessary to arrest Hurst is unknown. His history, as we now know it, was this. He was married, as a young man, to a Shropshire girl of only modest fortune and advantage. It does not appear that it was an unequal match socially, but they were neither of them wealthy. That marriage became unhappy and Hurst was reported to be frequently from home. Shortly after he married, he was the unexpected beneficiary of the estate of his late aunt. The apparently frustrated and aspirational Mr. Hurst had inherited a lot of money in his own right, and with it, his life changed. The rest, as they say, is history. His absences from home grew longer and his return journeys fewer and farther between. One day he left and did not return. Mrs. Hurst was to all intents and purposes abandoned, and her family outraged.

What they did not know, but must somehow have discovered, was that on 21 November 1810, the already married Mr. Hurst purported to take another wife. Miss Louisa Bingley was a well-placed society lady with significant wealth of her own. Since Hurst was independently wealthy, it is not clear why he married Louisa Bingley. Whatever the motivation, Mr. and Mrs. Hurst lived between his London home and her relations. The victim, of the first Meryton murder, Edwin Turnerville was the brother of the first Mrs. Hurst and it has been speculated that he was blackmailing the bigamist Hurst. In a turn of events worthy of a detective novel, Turnerville had, prior to his death, passed on incriminating information to another, who, wishing to test the water, but not with his own skin, had passed it to the Reverend Mr. William Collins. The unfortunate Mr. Collins revealed this information to Mr. Hurst and thereby sealed his own fate. Mr. Hurst was apprehended in Meryton, some two months after the second murder. He was never convicted, having taken his own life whilst in custody.

Where do the Meryton Murders take us in our analysis of Allwood? Well, here is another example of pursuing criminality wherever it may lie, of bringing down the highborn villain. It also suggests a systemisation in Allwood's methods of investigation, together with a willingness to work at a problem over an extended period of time. It is a sad fact that surprisingly little information about the case has survived. This is mostly due to Hurst having died before trial. However, it also appears, that although the case drew understandable public interest, Allwood himself sought to downplay it.

Thirdly, there are several references in the information logs at 4 Bow Street to visits there by Allwood throughout the 1820s—this despite the fact that he was resident in and a magistrate in Hertfordshire. To the systemisation noted above, therefore, I add connectedness. This was a man who gathered information and shared it.

Fourthly, and maybe less impressively, Allwood was involved in 1835 case of Esme Cook, a young seamstress who was found dead on a country lane near Hitchin. He was criticised heavily in the press for having suspected Miss Cook's betrothed, a young man who turned out to be innocent. It was said that while Allwood concentrated on him, the real killer, a dispossessed robber who had come upon the victim by chance, got away. Allwood did catch up with the offender, but only after he had murdered another young woman in the neighbouring county of Cambridgeshire. Allwood faced vitriolic criticism for this lapse in judgement and were it not for his defence by a number of prominent gentleman, including, rather oddly, the cousin of the then Earl of Matlock, a Mr. Fitzwilliam Darcy, his career may have ended there (I say "oddly" as Darcy was by no means local and nothing is known of how he came to know Allwood at all).

So, there you have the bones of it.

Could he be the precursor to the great British Detective? I leave it with you.

Finis.

ACKNOWLEDGMENTS

Thank you to Christina Boyd of The Quill Ink for your patient and meticulous work on the manuscript, boundless enthusiasm and friendship. When I decided to write a murder mystery in the present tense, I never imagined how many errors I would make. Thank you for correcting them with such good humour without ever losing the spirit or the shape of the story. You saved this book from the shredder and enhanced it many times over - thank you.

To Susan of CloudCat Design—thank you for the beautiful cover and putting up with my endless questions and pinterest misadventures.

To Beau for your formatting - and always being there to have a read and share ideas. You are a great writer and friend, thank you.

To Claudine for all of your help in promoting this and other stories. You are a real star.

Other writerly and readerly friends, who have helped me (in no particular order): Karen, Linda B, Caitlin, Joana, Lory, Elizabeth A, Rita D, Ana D, and Rosie Amber. Thank you also to all of the contributors to *The Darcy Monologues* and *Dangerous To Know*—it has been great to work with you all this last year.

Lastly, thank you to my family in particular my mum, who makes this possible in many ways, my lovely children who have no idea that I write stories and my husband, who is my most discerning critic.

ABOUT THE AUTHOR

Jenetta James is a mother, lawyer, writer, and taker-on of too much. She grew up in Cambridge and read history at Oxford University where she was a scholar and president of the Oxford University History Society. After graduating, she took to the law and now practises full-time as a barrister. Over the years, she has lived in France, Hungary, and Trinidad as, well as her native England. Jenetta currently lives in London with her husband and children where she enjoys reading, laughing, and playing with Lego. She is the author of *Suddenly Mrs. Darcy* and *The Elizabeth Papers*, and has contributed stories to the anthologies *The Darcy Monologues* and *Dangerous To Know: Jane Austen's Rakes and Gentlemen Rogues.*

Printed in Great Britain
by Amazon